Malaparte in Jassy

Malaparte in Jassy

Samuel Astrachan

Wayne State University Press   Detroit   1989

Library of Congress Cataloging-in-Publication Data

Astrachan, Samuel.
   Malaparte in Jassy / Samuel Astrachan.
      p.   cm.
   ISBN 0-8143-2162-3 (alk. paper)
   1. Malaparte, Curzio, 1898–1957, in fiction, drama, poetry,
   etc.   2. Iasi (Romania)—History—Fiction.   3. World War,
   1939–1945—Fiction.   I. Title.
   PS3551.S7M35   1989
   813′.54—dc19   89-30755
                                                                          CIP

This history of a series of events that took place in the town of Jassy in Romania during the Second World War is a fiction based on real events reported by Curzio Malaparte in his remarkable book *Kaputt.* I have dared meddle with his life, and with his reportages in *Kaputt* and in his book *The Skin,* but I have presented here only my own image of a man's sickness, of a world's sickness, of a man who becomes a witness.

One:

The Castle

1

I am sick. I live as if enclosed in glass, and there is no way of breaking through.

The Germans are gathering a hundred divisions at Stalingrad. But I am told privately that I have enemies and it would be wise for me to be someplace else. My dinner conversation has grown stale, my articles are suspect, Malaparte is again Mal à Propos.

I drive my two-door Ford back across Russia from the front. I sleep in abandoned ransacked houses infested with lice and bedbugs. There is only the Russian winter to kill the Russian vermin. The vermin have learned the Bolshevik tactics. They are partisan bandits, they attack from behind, they creep up on you at night. I take no prisoners, mercilessly I slap or squeeze them dead.

My muffler is pierced, the car coughs and explodes like a motorcycle. If I keep the windows closed, the heat becomes suffocating; if I open my window, dust from the road and from the vast arid abandoned fields blows into the car and I am caked in my pasty sweat with dust like sand. I work the windshield wipers but every now and then I must stop the car to clean the windows with a rag.

The motor overheats. A slender water line to the radiator has burst; with my pocketknife, I cut off the burst part and shorten the line.

On the narrow cramped back seat is my soldier's canvas bag, my holstered Beretta pistol, my small Certo Dolina camera, my typewriter. The typewriter broke in the winter. The metal was too tensile; one after the other the letters' arms cracked. I wear an Italian army sky blue uniform that has become gray for the dust and grime. I have the rank and privileges of a captain.

I drive day after day and cross the river Prut into Romania and now it is dusk and Jassy appears on its seven holy hills. The sun reflects off the golden cupolas and spires of its many churches. I see the tall shadowed buildings of the ghetto, where, for hundreds of years, cramped and enclosed by walls, the Jews added floor to floor until their narrow buildings seem to lean and hang over all the town.

A group of horsemen is riding from the town as if out of the sun; they raise the dust that is golden and blood red in the light; they sit their horses stiffly, they are gentlemen. Now I see leaping and racing in the dust about them a pack of lean dogs. They are training for the hunt.

2

It is a Brahms piano and string trio, the opening melody like a minuet. The music rises and descends, but it seems to ever grow more grave, a central voice longing. In a dance, we are on the verge of a darker presence.

The long high music room of the Jassy Jockey Club is crowded with the nobles and notables of Jassy. It is an early and awkward hour for evening dress, and those men who are not wearing military uniforms wear their informal English tweeds and flannels; most men are bearded or thickly mustached, some wear pince-nezzes, monocles; the women, however, wear long evening dresses, organdy, of pastel colors.

Folding chairs are arranged in lines, and some women and men lean slightly forward on their chairs to see and hear better. Some men stand by the high oak-paneled walls, their hands clasped behind them. Malaparte stands by a wall at the rear of the room. He is bullet-headed bald, he is head and shoulders taller than most of the nobles and notables of Jassy. Just inside the club doors, the jockey-small red-jacketed doorman, the features of his face thick and dwarflike, smiled up at him and very nearly winked as if he recognized or knew him, and brushed his skyblue uniform down.

The grand piano, its lid raised to resonate the sound into the room, stands in front of the giant empty fireplace. The pianist is a small pale unhealthy looking young man who plays bent low over the keyboard. The violinist is a German lieutenant, his fair face beautiful, like that of a messenger god. The gray-haired tall cellist alone squarely faces the auditors; there is something in his thin-lipped fine-featured face that Malaparte immediately likes, a glow like loyalty.

Malaparte sees out of the corner of his eye a framed print of a fishlike form. It is, he sees, a map of Romania, bass fish with its tail on the Black Sea, its body, beached on Bulgaria, pointing gaping into Europe. He thinks the beached fish is even blind, for, though the map does not show it, the Hungarians have taken that of Transylvania that would take from the fish its very eye. He will say at table to the stout beady-eyed nobles and notables of Jassy, You are someone's fish dinner, you are Germany's Lenten dinner. Among the nobles and notables are some who wear the operetta braided uniforms of Antonescu's German collaborating army, and some wear the black uniforms of Horia Sim's Iron Guard Milice. Framed in a full-length portrait high on the wall above the fireplace, staring out youthfully over all the room, is the new king, his high gold crown topped by a jeweled cross, his cape bordered with white ermine.

This is the more poignant dance of the second movement. It reaches, it yearns. It is the all but forgotten past, the sweetest moments of a life, and we are back in territories we shall never see again and perhaps that never were. Though the pale sickly pianist, in this piercing backwards yearning, makes us sense what has been put from mind, a coming chaos. The pianist is like a gnome bent over the piano, and, as in all bent figures, it is the angular that we see, the hooked nose, the chin that almost touches the keys. His hands are small and fine, woman's hands; his left hand rises sometimes above his ear and, before falling to the keys, hangs there an instant like something of him, or of the music, that exists in absence and echo.

Now, as we enter the chaos of the third movement, the gnomelike pianist is almost bouncing on his bench, and the cellist is fiercely bent over his instrument, and the beautiful violinist is sawing away fearfully, his mouth agape. It is a witches' sabbath, a release of demons. It grates on the ear, it is moving toward an unending screeching cry. The conclusion, reaching for order, is inadequate. Too much has been said, and it is perhaps for that, for what the pianist gave that might have been too personal an approach, or, it occurs to Malaparte now, intuiting, smiling, too racial an approach, that there is but casual applause. The nobles and notables of Jassy, and their wives, daughters, and mothers, clap with the tips of their fingers.

Countess Dimitriu is approaching from the front of the room, men and women bowing back out of her way. There is a soft glow about her, the silver hair, the gray eyes, her loosely flowing, tightly bodiced, crepe-aged and shadowed white gown, the silver shoes one sees only the small tips of.

Her daughter Elena, slightly taller than she, as slender, follows some steps behind. She wears a hundred-eyed-and-buttoned mourning gown. The skin of her proud face is dark and drawn tight.

Malaparte has not seen the countess or Elena since he was a young foreign correspondent in Poland where Count Dimitriu was Romanian ambassador to the court of Marshal Pilsudski. That was twenty years before, and Elena was fifteen, and, like a boy, rode in all the hunts.

The countess stops by Malaparte and smiles sideways at him. "Isn't it wonderful?" she asks as if it were only yesterday that they last met. Still, every question addressed to him is like a challenge.

He says, "The worse the world goes, the better the music."

She has not attended to his reply, or only to the manner and lilt of it. "Dear Curzio," she says, already continuing on her way, "you'll stay with us, of course."

3

The full moon is mist-veiled and aureoled; the moonlight pales the stony fields and orchards that slope this way and that. Peasants have been soldiers now for two years, and the thick old orchard trees, regularly spaced in long rising and falling lines, hang heavy with untrimmed branches, their shrinking leaves like wizening plums.

Malaparte's headlights are unnecessary to see the narrow sometimes pitted dirt road. The car is tall and, muffler coughing, leans this way and that. It is late. He looked vainly for the Italian Consul; he is, he was told, in Bucharest and will not be back for a week. There were no rooms available in the Jockey Club. He knows that the countess will not be waiting dinner for him, but he sees—looking ahead at the road, the sloping fields—a long table with dinner dressed men and women. He knows that the count is dead, but he sees him approaching him, tall as he, narrower, his broad-mouthed smile. 'You are suffering, my dear Malaparte, from a loss of affect. But we shall fix that!'

He is suspicious of the ghost. 'Dimitriu, I've been far.'

'I know, but now you're home.'

'I'm sick, Dimitriu, and you, you're dead.'

'What's a friend for, Malaparte, if you can't call him back from the dead?'

'We have friends to betray them.'

He is alone. He sees the top of tall trees soft against the aureoled moon-misted sky. The castle appears broad and still, almost at the edge of the forest; the castle towers rise pale like arms.

He parks his Ford by a clump of oak trees. Every time he turns the ignition key off, he wonders if the car will start up again. Inside the castle walls a dog is barking, and now several dogs are barking. He carries his heavy canvas soldier's bag. He crosses a thick plank drawbridge over a deep dry moat to the great looming carriage portals, and even as he is reaching to the bell cord, a servant opens the step-through door cut into one of the portals. The servant is so bald and tall that Malaparte thinks for an instant that he is himself.

"*Domnule* Malaparte?" the servant questions, his voice shrill.

Malaparte inclines his head ironically.

The servant stands immobile. He seems to be listening to far off forest sounds. "It's nothing," he says. The shrillness is the nature of his voice. He is calm. His face is smooth and hairless.

The large courtyard slopes up in dark gleaming rounded cobblestones toward the high looming inner face of the castle. Malaparte, following the servant who carries his heavy bag, sees parked in deep shadows a military motorcycle pulled up off its rear wheel. A brown and white mutt, strong hunting dog, leaves the other still growling dogs and comes sniffing after Malaparte. The dog leans toward him in that searching gesture between friendship and enmity, and Malaparte reaches familiarly down to pat the dog, the broad neck all of muscle. The dog rubs itself briefly against his leg over the top of his calf-covering boot and then yawns. Malaparte sees above in leaded windows the dim glow of a candle; he thinks he glimpses a woman's slender form standing by a window. The servant is half-turned, leaning slightly with the weight of the bag, waiting.

Inside the castle, the servant carries a candle, its long flame flickering. Distances are strange. Malaparte senses passages impossibly long, high-ceilinged room after high-ceilinged room. It is chilly, the damp of deep stone walls. At a doorway, the servant nods toward the center of a long table where some platters are set and napkin covered. The servant leads him up a broad stairway and through a broad corridor to a bedroom. The bed was made for a man his size. The servant lays the bag down and opens a large looming wardrobe and indicates, offering, the clothes within as he earlier indicated the setting at the table.

Now he is alone, a candle lit behind him on the dresser, his hand touching a tweed jacket, flannel trousers. These are the clothes of Dimitriu. They will be tight at the shoulders but will be the right length. He thinks of the count's long head hunched over his body, the eagle hook to his nose, the heavy-lidded eyes, the high cheekbones over the drawn cheeks. "Your professional hunch," Malaparte once joked, because the count was a medical doctor who had studied with Charcot and continued his gynecological studies even when he was a diplomat. "Which eye is the hypnotist? The right one, the left one, or the long vertical one in the middle?"

Malaparte strips and sets a large porcelain basin that was on the dresser onto the wood floor; he pours water from a tall pitcher into it. It is cold water, well water recently drawn. He cups his hands and brings water to his broad hairy chest. He squats over the basin; he washes in his crotch and in the middle body's weightlessness, his member begins to rise.

He is standing before the mirror. He breathes in, and no one has so broad and massive a chest, and the curling hair on the flowing curves of his chest is a forest, and who can wrestle him down! Below the chest is the bulging vertical abdominal muscle, the center of the body that painters rightly made radiant. And below the hardly softer but flatter horizontal abdomen is his manhood; his thighs are massive columns, pedestals of his body. Suddenly, he whirls around. There is only the wall behind him. He raises the candle to examine the wood paneling; built into the wall is a small door. There is no key in the keyhole. Surely there are hidden servants' passages and stairways linking every room in the castle.

He is a big man in silk, tweed, and flannel coming down the broad stone stairway of this castle and there is no light but what he carries in his hand, and what does he care about spying shadows! In the Bruhl Palace in Warsaw, white-flowing-haired Paderewski, president of the Polish nation, sits down at the grand piano and in the holy silence of the shared vision plays Chopin's *Funeral March,* the fervor of the consumptive, bared by the great pianist of all that could be personal, become an anthem. And the dinner-coated diplomats, and the tall dress-uniformed military attachés, stand attentive behind the chairs of their ambassadors and their ambassadors' wives and daughters, everyman's manner that before scorn, the very brink of godhood, the gods' music. He will breakfast alone at Capri at his Mon Repos—his very tower and aerie, built with the money of ten successes, of reportages, of smart moves—, on his terrace overlooking his debutante and starlet guests, his painters, writers, and politicians at their table by the rippling clear blue water of the swimming pool; the women's hair is cut short, boyish; he sees the little curls before the ears that are called *accroche-coeurs.*

He takes his place at the long table. There is Bordeaux; he pours the red wine; he raises the fine bowled glass, he bows his head to the wine's bouquet. He uncovers a platter, a broiled chicken is cut evenly in halves. He has still not tasted the wine. Is he afraid that the wine has turned, that the chicken is spoiled? The wine is clear; he sips it and even as the body of it slips down his throat, its touch soft and light, the soul of it rises doubly, through his ciliated nostrils receiving over the bowled glass, through the roof of his mouth, to the passages of his brain. He is carving and eating the bird now, and the mind of him is but a faint awareness of what his hands are doing, a deeper awareness of the mastication of the bird, the taste of the broiled but still moist meat of it, the bird descending. He pauses and sips the clear deep red wine.

He leaves a bit of wine in the bottle, a drumstick, princely gesture that whoever clean up partake. He puts a cigarette in his mouth, he strolls. There are oil portraits in the passage. The count was descended of heroes for Romanian independence; they fought the Turks, the Magyars. And before that his people fought the Mongols, and before that his people had been the mysterious Dacians who had fought off the Celts but had adopted the Roman way so thoroughly their Romanian language is the purest daughter of Latin.

He pauses and lights the cigarette with his candle, and in the changed glow of light he sees in a niche in the oak-paneled passage wall a dull gleaming bronze sculpture of twin heads.

These are ancient death masks, the gaze inwards, forward and backward Janus heads hooked together as if by a bone. The lidded eyes are longer and fuller than eyes can be, they contain. Still, it is Dimitriu's own high-cheekboned broad-mouthed face. There is a rising bursting at the lidded eyes, as at the lips, as at the bone joining the heads, that is really a containing, and in each head the left eye is lower than the right. There is a secret beneath the language the Romanians speak, beneath their Eastern Orthodox faith. He has seen these bronze heads in his mind like a projection before a city, and in the stone walls of the city are the skulls of men. The cigarette between his lips is lit, the smoke is in his mouth. He is facing the bicephalus, and he knows the smoke will be bad, German, spoiled, that the spoiling will even seep back in time and space and the wine and chicken will be spoiled in his body and mind.

He stands in the open doorway of a high-ceilinged sitting room. There are two wingback chairs facing glowing embers in the fireplace, and between the chairs is a chessboard table, large hand-filling black and white ivory pieces in position.

"I'd like to play," he says, smiling thinly, "but I'm only a beginner."

"I haven't played in years," a voice answers from one of the chairs, and he is only faintly surprised, a heavily lipsticked blond woman wearing a bright red gown, her French tinged with a German accent, guttural at the r's and v's, leaning to face him from behind a wing of the chair. She is thin; he can tell she is almost as tall as he.

"Malaparte!" he says, inclining his head.

She smiles that she knows.

Her overly lipsticked mouth is long, the top lip and overbite rabbitlike. Her hair is long and soft and touches her bare shoulders. He suspects she stands with a careless hunch.

Her long red gown grips the tops of her small breasts, cutting there. A sixteen-year-old girl might dress this way. But she is thirty. She has heightened the color of her cheeks with rouge, her eyes are underscored with green pencil.

"Still, I'm not a bad player," she says and he smiles. He has always been amused by women who compete at men's games. He senses then that she put on this red dress for his sake and he begins to frown.

He sits in the wingback chair across the chess table from her. He looks at the hand-carved pieces; each is different. A white knight is reining in his horse. He picks up a black soldier pawn and a white one. He brings them behind his back and then holds out his closed fists. She touches his fist, her finger is long, the fingernail painted red; he opens his hand on the white pawn. She smiles at her advantage.

She plays king's gambit, he plays his intuition. He opens up the center of the board by a pawn move and instantly his bishop is in her king's corner; he is prepared to sacrifice bishop for pawn and position; but she will be smarter and holds back the exchange. He checks her king; his knight sweeps in for a second check; and then, swiftly, he begins a sequence, in which she is always one move behind, to have her castle. She is pale and angry, she bites her lip. He captures her castle. He must withdraw his bishop and knight, he wants to open a line forward for his queen to attack. But he begins to realize how over-extended he is. She is beating upon his unformed defensive positions, every move forward an attack on a piece, a structuring of vectors toward his king.

The red gown bites into the smooth firm flesh at the tops of her small breasts; there is something insectlike about her long body. She smiles with her overbite.

She says, "Your guardian angel told me I might see you here. He asked me to greet you for him."

He has castled as if for delaying.

And suddenly again she pales seeing that she has fallen into a trap. Her hand darts forward to bring back the white soldier pawn she has just advanced, but her hand ceases, she seeing in his manner and in his smiling eyes that he would even permit that.

"I've many guardian angels."

"You're very lucky!"

"Once, I had a string of guardian angels a hundred kilometers long."

"Will you play another?"

There is a look in his eyes when he tells a story, the story more real than the present moment.

"We were going to the Smolensk front. I was in the command car leading the column. Snow was falling so thickly we could hardly see. I thought we were lost. Then I noticed that the driver and the commander bundled in the rear at my side were looking this way and that for signs. Suddenly, astonishing like an apparition, we came upon a soldier directing traffic. There he was, in the middle of nowhere, in the middle of a blizzard, planted up to his chest in a snowbank, pointing the way.

" 'How,' I asked when I had seen a second and a third man standing pointed in the snow, 'can men stand out there directing traffic?'

" 'We Germans,' the commander said, 'can transform anything. We take Russians and make them into angels! Our guardian angels! It's not difficult. The secret is: Wait till they freeze! Because then, when you lift an arm, it will point all winter long!' "

She is smiling at him but as if she has already heard the story, as if he and not what he has recounted is at issue.

He is lying on his bed in the tall-ceilinged dank room and he cannot sleep. He should not have eaten. It is the chicken, it is the wine, it is turning and rising in him now. Distantly, he hears a longing music. He sees himself uniformed, booted, in a room of women, holding the fair slender girl's hand.

'What's your name?' he coaxes.

'I have no name.'

His fingertips touch the curl of her *accroche-coeur*.

'Do they treat you well?'

'We are like princesses here.'

'Then your name is Sarah. Sarah, why are you so sad?'

'I can't tell you.'

'It's as if you were under a spell.'

She is crying and something crazy is happening to her face, the child's face melting, liquefying. . . .

He is kneeling on the floor over the chamber pot. He is in his mind holding a chicken by its stick legs upside down. He pulls at its neck to be able to cut its carotid, and he sees then a thousand tiny white worms at its pink anus. The retch is rising with bile to his throat, but every time he opens his mouth to release it hot and pouring, it is as if something in him but separate from him rises and with yawning open jaws swallows the retch back down.

There is no end to it. He is kneeling on the floor before the chamber pot and he is dry retching and it is tearing his body apart, and suddenly a warm hand is on his damp cold forehead. He looks up and he sees in dim flickering candlelight as if from beneath the surface of water a large dark servant woman looking with pity at him, her head cocked to a side. Her lips are thick; her breasts are large, rising with feeling.

"*Domnule* captain," she says, and then speaks on in her soft language, consoling, enveloping mother tongue he cannot now grasp. She helps him to rise. But now he stands towering over her and he takes her shoulders in his hands. She begins to tremble and now he is forcing her body to his, and he is bending to her and pressing his still wet lips to hers.

"*Domnule* captain!" she calls softly, urgently. "*Domnule* captain, no! *Domnule* captain, no!"

But he has fallen her across the bed, and his legs are spread wide over hers, his thighs pinning hers, his hand pulling amid thighs at her clothes and his, and now his member is entering her, and she moans, "No," and his middle body is rising and then thrusting down, and she is receiving, writhing, and then rising to his rising.

"Marynona! Marynona!"

Malaparte turns to the open door of the servants' passage and sees there a childlike face shriveled in a drinker's grin.

"*Domnule* captain, let me go! let me go!" Her head is tossing wildly, her body twisting and writhing to receive him deeper.

"Marynona! Marynona!"

Malaparte stands searching in a crouch inside the cold, low, narrow, and unlit servants' passage. In his bedroom, the massive servant woman is softly crying. The sound of footsteps is receding above, the music is coming from above. He climbs in a crouch a tight winding stairway, there is barely room for his booted feet on the steps. The air is getting cooler. He emerges outside the inner walls into the moonlight, he facing then out over a battlement the moonlit white mist-covered forest. The music has ceased, he is looking into the mist-covered forest, silence deeper than music.

He hears in the forest an owl hooting, and far off, like answering its call, is the high shriek of a fox. He sees in his mind the owl motionless on a branch of a tree, he sees its hawklike dropping onto a prey, its tearing at its neck. He wants to enter the forest now as if it, or something in it, makes him afraid. He wants to penetrate the depths of the forest now as if it too hides from him his own secrets. He is standing with his back to the tower facing the mist on the forest that is like a white covering sea reaching enveloping vapors even to the castle. But here, in a wall behind him, is a glow of golden light. It is a slit in the wall, archer's window called a "murderer." He leans to the slit that broadens as it deepens and sees in a shadowy candlelit tall deep room the young German officer he saw earlier playing violin in the trio, and, smiling in a far corner, red-dressed, her legs akimbo like an athlete resting, watching, the tall blond knowing woman with whom he played chess. And now he sees the long slender hundred-eyed-and-buttoned black-dressed form of Elena approaching the German.

The German is leaning back in a low-backed straight armchair, his head thrown back, his eyes closed; his legs are stretched forward, his hand trailing the violin and bow on the floor as if he has only just stopped playing. His fair silken hair is damp, his smooth face, the fine proud boyish features, is tense yet with striving, a longing music receding beyond his grasp. Elena kneels to him. Her hair is dark, tight to her head, her cheekbones are high, broad above the narrower lower face. Her body seems not to move, her head reaching forward. She reaches her long slender hand to the German's and brings it to her lips. The hand of the young violinist is trembling and Elena kisses, at the point of her lips, each fingertip, and her large unblinking eyes are steady on him, and Malaparte reads in her eyes the admiring love of this boy god, desire, but mockery too, and he sees the broader mockery in the face of the blond red-dressed akimbo-legged tall woman. Now, Elena's eyes close, and the sinking of the lids over her eyes is a veiling, is a taking all within, she as if eyes within the caverns of her body, and even now she takes the tip of a finger of the trembling young German officer into her lips, and, her lips like a thousand pursing and releasing muscles of a single muscle, she is kissing it within her mouth, a look now on her eyelidded face of the ecstasy that is like small pain.

Malaparte will walk in the night. The bile is again rising to his mouth as he crosses the cobblestone court-yard. The brown and white hunting dog that earlier came to rub against his leg is immediately with him, and, when he opens the step-through door in one of the carriage portals, the dog leaps joyously through. Now, in the field behind the castle that rises to the forest, the dog runs playfully to and from Malaparte, making bounding leaps, appearing and disappearing in the high wet grass, and there is a hesitation like memory in Malaparte, and he bends to still and caress the dog, and then rubs deeply, like his own thigh, the dog's massive neck. If this dog were to sink his teeth into an enemy, no man could pull him loose. His name is Loyalty, Prince, Soldier. "Stay!" he commands, memory becoming image. The dog immedi-ately sits back on its haunches in the field, its eyes beg-garlike and sad.

He is alone, the dog obedient behind, crossing the rising field to enter the forest, and the bottoms of his pants already have grass and wildflower parts stuck to them, and in his mind he sees gray-green uniformed soldiers kneel-ing, some leaning on their upright rifles, in a spread-out line about the edge of a forest, and from within the forest come the sounds of soldiers clacking metal on metal to beat their prey before them, the barking of their dogs.

25

And now, out of the forest, come tens of leaping rabbits, and the German soldiers here, their rifles at the ready, smile them through, and a hundred low flying whirring birds, and a deer that bounds high and beautiful like something from a dream except that growing and crescendoing behind it are the sounds of clacking metal and the yelping and as if biting dogs. One of the soldiers here calls out, "Here come the mice!" They come stumbling, running, disheveled girls, small boys, a hatted bearded man in a long black satin coat, low to the ground, the soft furry furtiveness indeed of mice, and the Germans here taking aim.

'Why, Malaparte, do your stories always end at the same point, the point of suspense?'

He will not look at the hypnotist. It is his own voice, it is only in his head.

He is tall and big and bullet-headed, but he is dwarfed by the forest, and the taste of bile in his mouth has become nausea in his belly, and there is a looseness in the muscles of his bowels and a pressure at his sphincter, all his body lowering, loosening, toward the ground. He thinks, and smiles, that it is only the bowels of him that have hypnotized him here. The trees are tall spruce and birch; they do not branch until high on their trunks where, tree to tree, they begin to weave a thickening net that holds the wet and dew down in a silvery mist. He walks on the loamy forest floor of rotting leaves, twigs, and limbs. Giant fern hangs like lace over the multitudinous luxuriant rotting undergrowth. He sees huge fallen trees. Their turned up roots are Medusas' heads, they are long-backed beasts melting, they are horses caught and frozen in a wave and foam frozen sea, the great eyes, the vast grin-twisted expanse of toothed smile.

'It makes you the only subject of your story. The tension is in you witnessing what you then do not describe, in you feeling what you do not, as if it would be unbearable, describe.'

He is advancing into the forest and again he feels he is being watched. The owl is watching him from the branch of a tree, the trees themselves are living birds, a raven's sharp-beaked head compacted on a coiled snake; the big winged eagle, an upward surging whalelike fish. He is squatting low and bare to the loam, he is gigantic and the trees are unending; he is miniscule and the trees soar out of sight in a shadowy glow above. He is peeing forward, the other rottenness turning in his belly, descending, gurgling liquid. He sees by a rotting tree trunk finger-high white mushrooms; they push up from the loam like monster excrescences born of it, their white stems fat and soft, their caps umbrellaing out in smooth sponges whose underbellies are networks of a thousand tiny wet breathing absorbing cells. His bowels are releasing, steaming into the loam; the draining of him does not stop, the poisons coming from so far; they wash out in gigantic explosions of gas and liquid, and even then his stomach is turning in spasms upward. His sight fails, his body is retching forward and backward, huge poisoned inhabited thing, and almost rising in him is the source of all poison that he dare not see, transposing words only almost coming to mind, *anus* is one.

Here the forest is very dense and dark and he walks, emptied of rot, light like a spirit, weak. These are giant gnarled thick live oaks, massive trunks sometimes elbowing up, great limbs hanging horizontally above, a wild disorder in the growth of trunks and branches. The bark of these trees is lizard wrinkled, ancient leather, and here and there in the leather are living swirls like frozen eyes. These trees are never bare and the mass of small pointed leaves, branches and limbs twisting, convoluting, knotting to reach the sky, is almost impenetrable, and it is a dying moonlit penumbra here where rain can hardly fall and where the loam is ever wet. Root ends of the live oaks appear here and there in the black loam like running bleeding veins, but the loam is such that no other plant can take root, the loam itself rich and alive, powerful, burning.

Malaparte hears a brief sound like a snort. In the dark silvery distance is a giant black boar. Horseback, Malaparte has charged boar that, bayed by dogs, have, short-legged, hurtled themselves forward to receive the point of his lance in the no-neck space behind their pointed ears, but this razor-backed wild boar's body is huge beyond any he has ever seen. Now, as if suddenly aware of his presence, the beast looks up. Its bulging eyes are fiery red. It raises its wet-snouted head, its tusks sweeping up, and it groans, the sound rising long, astonishing, shrill, as if from deep out of the loam. And as if the beast exhaled it, Malaparte smells suddenly a cesspool stink. Even then the beast is gone. Malaparte approaches where the beast was. It has everywhere dug its wet snout into the loam, and there it worked its obscenely cloven feet into the loam as if to return all its body into it, and there it wallowed angrily, longingly, in the giving wet surface. He wants to cup the earth up in his hands to bring it closer yet. But then he smiles, remembering a story. Peasants say that when a woman is in a forest and comes upon a wild boar, she has only to raise her skirt and squat for the boar to turn its path from her.

Malaparte turns and there, waiting big-eyed on its

haunches as if he only happened to be here, is the spotted hunting dog.

"You are disobedient, Prince," Malaparte says caressingly, naming him.

4

When he awakes, it is early afternoon. His uniform is gone; his boots have been cleaned, polished to a high shine; the flannel pants and tweed jacket he wore have been brushed down and are laid out neatly over the back of a chair. He dresses, thinking he will visit a day or two with the countess and Elena and be on his way. He will drive west across the lowlands into Yugoslavia; he will cross Croatia using Pavelic's safe-conduct pass—'my good friend, Malaparte'—and in Italy will phone Ciano and the foreign affairs minister will have him, his collar raised, his hat brim shading his eyes, guided swiftly down the boot of Italy to Naples where he will embark on the ferry to Capri.

He must put on paper all he has seen and lived. Who else has seen so much! He can be master again, he can triumph again, but he must have it all clear in his mind. He must contain it, he must shape it.

In the long room at the long table where Malaparte, the night before, ate alone the chicken and drank the rich red wine, the silver-haired countess and Elena sit with their guests, or whom Malaparte thinks are their guests. They have finished the midday meal and are at coffee.

There is no fire in the fireplace and it is cool and damp, and there is no light but distant leaded windowed daylight, and half the pride of castle people is to live elegantly in the dark and cold. They allow themselves fires in the evening. They have fine oriental carpets, but as if only to enhance the flagstoned floors. The women have wardrobes of thick sweaters and furs, they wear the skins of beasts made into long buttonless vestments over finer clothing. Their eyes are large, Byzantine, unblinking. The tips of their noses are red, there is a blueness at their lips, which barely move when they smile or speak. They know what they want, they are served in their every desire; and yet there is sometimes something about them like children sucking in their cheeks and puckering their lips to seem well behaved.

The countess's hand in Malaparte's—he taking it to his lips—is soft as a girl's. Still, there is a touch of rouge in her cheeks. She has had a drink or two, wine with her meal.

Elena too gives her hand to Malaparte. The skin of her face is tight and tanned as if she emerged from the sun and sea. All her artifice is to appear unadorned, and her manner, he thinks, is to be—even as he has thought he is sick—affectless. She is no longer a young woman, she is beginning that middle age of perfection that some women can maintain twenty years. He remembers her face the night before, the pursed mollusk lips. He remembers suddenly, startlingly close for an instant, her face when she was a girl. She was not pretty then, his eyes staring into hers, the pores of her skin; she had no manner but only pride and fire, her long bony body then against his.

A long-legged narrow-headed greyhound is at her feet.

The countess introduces the woman with whom Malaparte played chess as Pauli. She wears today a tight gray tunic and matching pants like a uniform, a gray kerchief ties her ash blond hair close to her head. Her manner is as severe as her clothes; still, there is red polish on her long fingernails and there is a moistness at the corners of her lips. There is a softness as of childhood in the fair and silken-haired young German officer whose name is Rainer.

An Iron Guard cross-belted black-uniformed young man, eighteen or nineteen years old, is Patrice. He has the self-satisfied look that Malaparte knows is merely the mask covering the smoldering dissatisfaction of he who disappoints. His face is covered with acne. But now, as Malaparte looks more closely at him, he is troubled seeing in the boy's face the fleeting childlike face that spied on him last night, but also the high proud cheekbones of a Dimitriu. He understands then that Elena is wearing black not for her father but for a husband. The boy is Elena's son. He heard of her marriage, he recalls, just after he frequented the Dimitriu in Warsaw. He carelessly counts the years, it seems to fit.

He goes to take the place that is waiting for him at the other end of the long dark table from the countess.

"You shall eat, Curzio," the countess says, "and we shall, waiting for your news, entertain you with gossip and stories. Though all my stories begin with, 'Do you remember. . . .' "

"Only coffee," Malaparte says to the woman servant of the night before who stands in shadows by a sideboard at a wood-paneled wall. He says to the countess, "I had word from Axel Munthe that the Americans bombed Capri. They were aiming for Rome, but they got lost on the way."

Everyone is smiling.

"Munthe says that my house was touched."

"I'm so sorry," the countess says, moved.

"Munthe is almost blind," Malaparte says and almost sees the tall man seated bent over himself. "He took from the rich and gave to the poor," he says, it not mattering at all how much he believes what he says. The world-famous author was a society doctor in Paris, London, and Rome and built his house, like Malaparte, on Capri.

"He loved all animals," the countess says.

"It's true, we've all loved animals. The last time I saw him, he'd moved into his tower and taken up knitting. I made him cry telling him of the suffering of animals."

The countess speaks of a friend who has become a Sister of Charity. The son of a Polish friend was killed leading a cavalry charge. Their friends' nicknames are Bunny, Muffy.

The servant is leaning toward him to pour the thick coffee into a demitasse. There is a faint mustache fuzz over her lip.

It is real coffee, the oriental density that one does not stir, the first sips bitter and then faintly sugared, and then the sweetened mass at the bottom.

"I've not had such coffee in months. No," he says, "that's not true. Every German commanding generl has his own kitchen and purveyor, and every collaborating official has German privileges, and I've dined with them all."

There is understanding and pity in the countess's gray eyes. She says, "Had you come to visit when *he* was alive, then you would have been a guest. We had everything. Now all we have left is Marynona and Inre."

Elena explains, "Inre is my mother's provider. He says," and she pitches her voice solemnly high in imitation, " 'I serve only God and the Dimitriu.' "

"It sounds like a motto," Malaparte says.

"Do you know ours?" Elena asks. "A lion is roaring, and, underneath, is written on a banner, '*Noli me tangere.*' 'Don't touch the lion.' I think my father was embarrassed by it. It's nowhere here to be seen."

"Your father," the countess corrects, "was never embarrassed by anything."

"He would be embarrassed now," Malaparte says. "His king has lost not only his coat of arms, but all his clothes. The king should at least have a motto. He might wear it as a figleaf. '*Achtung!*' could be his motto.

Pauli says, "Perhaps all the naked king is afraid of is being touched."

"Pauli," the countess says, "is here to catalogue us. Like all Germans, she thinks we're a barbarian people."

"What an idea!" Pauli protests. "Jassy, everyone knows, is the Jerusalem of the Balkans. And now that Malaparte is here, it shines as brightly as Paris or Rome."

"Berlin is the new center of the world," Elena says.

"I'm here," Pauli explains, "to photograph Romanian rites."

"Marynona," Patrice says turning, and asks now in the dialect, his voice deepening as a boy's becomes a man's, "what do the people do when they think the hand of God is turned against them?"

Everyone is looking at Marynona lost in shadows. She is shaking her head that she will not answer, that he should not ask.

"What do they do?" Patrice taunts, voice of a man, coaxing manner of a child.

Malaparte's gaze is lost in Marynona, and it seems to him that within her large hairy darkness, in the way she is breathing No, are other voices, deep gathering forces.

Malaparte asks, "Was that not German music I heard last night?"

"It was Brahms," the young German officer, Rainer, answers.

"I can never listen to Brahms without blushing," Malaparte says.

"I should like to see you blush," Elena says.

"I'm blushing now."

"It's Brahms' introspection and melancholy that affects us so," Rainer explains.

Elena says, "Marco makes the music more introspective than it is, more moody."

But Rainer is shaking his head. "With Brahms all excitement is interior, is a fantasy, a fever."

"That even sounds like Marco," Elena says, and the German blushes. She reaches across the table to touch the boy's hand with hers. She says to Malaparte, "Don't you think they explain too much? They might leave music alone. There are things one does not want to learn about or explain but only do and feel."

Malaparte does not answer.

"When I first knew you," Elena says, "everyone read everything you wrote, everyone hung on your words. Some people called you 'our modern Machiavelli.' Everyone knew you'd been a hero in the war. I thought you were afraid of no one."

He is remembering the bony girl to whom he said, smiling, 'Pity, you'll never wear corsets.' "Malaparte," he says, "is a hero only like Max Schmeling."

"Then Malaparte is a Greek hero," says the photographer, smiling.

"Cretin," Malaparte corrects. "Schmeling, you know,

was wounded on Crete and Doctor Goebbels had him brought to Berlin to be a hero. They put him on the radio and asked, 'Max, how were you wounded?' They wanted an epic, a killing of Greeks. But Max is like me, we've been away from home too long, and too many Brown Bombers have knocked us out and scrambled our brains. Max said, 'I was parachuted onto the island and even as I got myself free, mortar shells were bursting all around us, and I heard one coming and dived for cover, and the next thing I knew I was hit in the rear and wet in the pants.' "

They are laughing. Schmeling is, after all, only a prizefighter.

"Doctor Goebbels wouldn't forgive him. They say Schmeling's on the Russian front even now. Though maybe, you'll say, the Russian front is the center of the world."

"That would make the center of the world a thousand kilometers long," Rainer says practically, smiling as if this mocking language is proof he is not embarrassed at being a German.

"Romanians are there, Hungarians, Bulgarians," Malaparte says. "An Italian division is there, French and Spanish volunteers. It's a crusade against bolshevism. And on the other side are Tartars, Mongols—Asia! It's the great battle at the marches of our civilization. Yes, surely the Russian front is the center of the world."

"Have you seen Pauli's work?" the countess asks.

"They are photographs of black Max Schmelings," Elena says.

"Then they are Joe Louis's."

"They are pure black wrestlers," Pauli says. "Their bodies are beautiful. Every part of them is pure living force. Every limb of them is beautiful in itself, more beautiful in the flowing moving whole." Elena smiles as if she has heard this before. "They've nursed wounds in the skin by their umbilicals into raised twined serpents." Malaparte thinks that the mocking irony in her eyes is really covering a glow of belief. He sees for an instant the hard glowing vertical abdominal muscle. "Now, in the hot flat day, two wrestlers squat in the sand and paint orange dye about their eyes. There are small camp fires in which the wrestlers burn a special wood, and they separate ash from the fire and wet themselves with ash. And now, like orange-dyed beasts risen from the ash, they face each other hunched forward."

She has stood and she bends now into the athlete's crouch—her gray uniformlike tunic and pants, her gray kerchief—, her hands on her thighs, the red spots of her fingernails, and she seems like a great tall preying insect; and Malaparte stands to face her, and he too has his hands on his thighs, and they begin to circle each other and their hands rise and spread at the level of their chests, and their circle, in the long dark room, turns and spirals them in, and Malaparte is facing her, and who is she, and with whom must he wrestle, and he makes a feinting lunge toward her, and everyone is laughing.

"I've only one rite left," the countess, smiling sadly, says when Malaparte and Pauli are again seated. "I sit at my table and play solitaire. Every card has a meaning."

"Every turned-over card," Malaparte says, "is like an old friend."

"Malaparte," Pauli asks, "are you the Tartar? Or are you the Crusader?"

"If the Crusader carried a cross, I'd be the Crusader."

"You're afraid of the swastika? It's only a wheel, a symbol of spiritual well-being."

36

"It's a wheel with hammers for spokes. No, I'm afraid of the cross."

"You're a mystifier, Malaparte."

"One cross, you see," he says, crossing his big fingers, "makes two gallows."

Pauli is laughing.

Elena says, "Malaparte has become a cynic."

"Don't insult your dog," Malaparte replies, and the long-legged narrow-headed dog, jealous of its mistress's attention, begins to rise.

"*Noli me tangere,*" Malaparte growls threateningly as the dog growls. And again there is laughter, though the cross-belted acne-faced boy is staring scornfully at the man growling at a dog.

The countess says gently, "Malaparte is hurt."

"Malaparte was a hero," Malaparte says, "but Malaparte is hurt. Malaparte would be a hero still, but the time we live in is like a bad dream and no man is a hero in his own bad dream."

"I smell a story," Pauli says.

"I am, let us say," Malaparte says, "a Luftwaffe fighter pilot. My plane has been hit and I am descending into a perfectly cloudless evening horizon. I am walking across the desert toward a setting flaming sun. The sand is caked, like a burned-out crust. Something has happened to me. Am I hurt? I look at my hands, they are changing, my hands are visibly aging. I do not understand what is happening or where I am. I have crash-landed on another planet where every minute is a year. I feel it now in my shortness of breath, I feel it in the thickness of the blood in my veins. I want to return to my plane, but it is gone. I don't know which way to go. Everywhere is only crusted desert and time is rushing at me."

37

"What a tedious story!" Pauli says.

"It is only a first version," Malaparte says.

The countess's high bedroom forms a turret-rounded corner of the castle. In the turret, where the countess, a drink in hand, sits waiting on a cushioned stone bench before a card table, are narrow leaded windows from which one can see the forest. Still, the light that enters the turret reaches only dimly into the large, high, otherwise windowless room. Malaparte smells paint. He glimpses, painted on gesso on the walls, ladies walking in garden lanes, gentlemen training falcons; he sees gentlemen on horses, lean hunting dogs even like Elena's. The very ceiling is painted, a starry sky. There is a blue radiance in all the room. He glimpses a scene of a deer chased by dogs. The deer is running frightened, her eyes astonished.

The countess's bed is canopied.

"He can go far," the countess says, and at first Malaparte does not understand. The boy. He can almost see the acne-faced boy in her eyes. "He needs a . . . friend, an advisor."

She is looking at him as if that is her request.

"You'll need a change of clothes," she says.

"He'll need a change of uniform. I need nothing," Malaparte says, though he is already wearing the count's clothes.

"Do you think so?" she says pondering as if he has given his first advice. "Do you think they've no future? You must speak with him, we must look into this. You see, he has nothing else for the moment," she says as if explaining her approbation, asking for his.

He says nothing.

"I never blamed you," she says, and he pales. "Oh,"

she says, remembering, "a message came for you this morning. Colonel Lupu wants to see you."

In his room, he sees a note half hidden under this pillow. It reads: "Leave my mother alone."

He smiles. The child is afraid, the child longs for. The child is afraid of what he longs for. Like a child, he could not decide to hide the note or leave it in the open. He thinks of the boy going through the servants' passages of the castle. He thinks of the boy spying always behind doors, in drawers. He is pacing the high dank room. He thinks that Elena has taunted the boy even as the boy taunts Marynona, that Elena laughs at the boy even as the countess consoles him. He again counts the years.

He is faint. He has lived all his life by a language of up and down, of winning and losing, and now he is losing, sinking. And suddenly he is afraid as if all about him forces were rising against him. A mirror! He needs a mirror! Of what am I afraid? Only of a boy! He is smiling into the mirror. I am who I am!

5

It is midafternoon and Malaparte walks down the dirt road that cuts between abandoned fruit tree orchards toward Jassy. He looked, in the cobblestoned castle courtyard, for Prince. "Here, Prince!" he called. But the dog did not come. "Here, Prince!" he called, walking among the dogs, sensing first a fear in them as if he carried a whip in his shadow, but then they turned away indifferently and some pushed and growled among themselves before the remainders of the slops thrown out to them on the cobblestones.

The motorcycle was gone. Malaparte thinks of the acne-faced boy, goggled, riding the motorcycle into Jassy on this road.

The regularly spaced orchard trees are losing their roundish wizened leaves; they are plum trees, the bark ravaged. There are limbs that have cracked with the weight of the hanging fruit, and yet, elbowing down, are still alive. The coming winter will snap them off.

The outlying houses of Jassy are tin-roofed, put together with planks of wood and sheets of tar paper. The wood has been recovered from crates, from other such houses, charred planks, planks gray with dirt, rotting. The houses are dilapidated before they are built; they are torn down, their parts stolen, in a night. The windows are often of greased and almost transparent newspaper, dated, headlined, GERMANS ADVANCING TOWARD ROSTOV, and newspapers crumpled and wetted with paste fill like plaster the holes between the planks and the tin roofs. Chickens scratch at the wet black earth before the houses, and here and there against a house is a stack of rotting branches gathered for firewood, guarded by dogs on leashes, by sharp-eyed women who all look like grandmothers, babushkas tight about their drawn faces.

Closer to the center, the wood houses are built one next to the other, and they are two, three, and four stories, and sometimes the upper floors push out on beams to overhang the narrow street, and sometimes the whole building is tilted and beams are pried into the street to hold the building up. Here men are selling used clothes. There are rows of hanging crammed-together worn jackets. Pants are thrown in piles, men pick the crumpled things up and hold them, studying, against their bodies. The shirts too are in piles, vast gray piles that men walk in. A shoemaker, sitting in front of his closet-small shop, is hammering tiny nails that he takes from between his lips into a leather sole. A thick oily smoke of cooking trails in the now crowded street. Malaparte sees glazed and bulging-eyed men carrying on their bent backs giant weights laid on platforms that are tied by leather slings to their foreheads. He sees a crowd of men and women before a three-portaled stone church crammed between wood buildings. On the steps outside are mitred and bearded popes wearing gold, silver, and jeweled encrusted vestments, and yet they are dirty, or seem dirty, their straggly beards, a fierce burning light in their eyes. Tonsured monks, their faces as smooth and hairless as women's, are waving smoking censers, the incense rising black. They are calling the people to Vespers, but their words themselves are like a service, and behind them, in the dark church, candles burn in red-glassed lanterns. "Are you a Christian?" a pope demands, and Malaparte hears the growing murmuring response, "We are Christians!" "Are you Christians or infidels?" "Father, we are Christians!" "Then scourge yourselves with the Holy Word!"

Malaparte has seen this many times, the bearded priests of Poland and Lithuania, the mad-eyed patriarchs who proudly greeted the conquering German troops in tar paper Russian villages.

"Colonel Lupu," Malaparte asks the dwarflike red-jacketed doorman at the crowded entry of the Jockey Club. Squabbling men fall silent and still as if time stops, and they resume their calling and insisting only after the doorman winks Malaparte in, indicating the broad stairway inside.

Malaparte glimpses in an open ground floor club room tables of gentlemen playing cards. One stout monocled player looks up at him and, then, returning his attention to his cards, speaks to the others. He climbs the stairway, the fittings here—balustrades, paintings, chandeliers—of a grand hotel, the rooms and suites here are all large, high-ceilinged, designed, fifty years before, that nobles and notables be at home when they come to Jassy. But the second floor suites and rooms have now been taken over by German and Romanian military and paramilitary services. Doors are open; there are few telephones and the different services must share the inadequate hotel equipment, junior officers going busily from one office to another. Malaparte thinks that the nobles and notables below keep their club room doors open to keep an eye on the comings and goings, the dealers who sell to the Germans, the lawyers who write the contracts, the new rich.

Upstairs in the corridor, too, people are waiting, pacing, every man in his rank, the lawyers bowing to underofficials, the dealers unctuous; the petitioners who represent only a son who has been drafted, a horse that has been requisitioned, wait uncomfortably, cap in hand, by the walls. Outside one office, Malaparte sees a handful of bearded hatted Jews. People stare at them unpleasantly. The Jews do not remove their hats, they stand in a dark group arguing among themselves.

"Sit down, Malaparte," Colonel Lupu says without looking up.

He is Malaparte's age, young colonel. He is well built but lacks height. His fair hair is cut short, it bristles. He has the soldier's look of pride, mission, competence, but something else, the grayness, depth, and cunning of those who work in Intelligence. A map of Europe and the Mediterranean basin is on the wall behind him.

Malaparte does not sit. He has been summoned, let

the other explain. Lupu is one of those, Malaparte thinks, who would make him feel like a strutting cock. Still, he senses now as Lupu looks up at him that Lupu wants other of him, that there is behind the quick mockery a searching regard.

"You come from the front, Malaparte. What's the situation?"

"The Pope's going to weep."

Lupu sits back. "He's going to weep for the Russians?" he asks, smiling, playing along.

"He hasn't wept for the French, the Poles, the Greeks. He hasn't wept for the Jews. No, the Father's going to weep for the son."

"I don't understand the joke."

"That's as much as you've paid me."

The colonel's face clouds, but then he nods. He says, "Everyday, German convoys pass through this region transporting troops and supplies to Russia. It's the greatest massing of troops in all history. The English, it's said, are secretly suing for peace. The Americans Lindbergh and Ford have always wanted good relations with Hitler. Look at the map! Everyone thinks the war will be over by spring."

"The problem is," Malaparte says, "there aren't enough Germans to go around." He stands tall in the count's tweed jacket and fine flannel pants, and he looks so often above the bristling hair of the colonel's head that the colonel will stand. He is thinking that the charm of these rooms, of these corridors and hotels, is spaciousness and accessibility, line of high rooms, door after door. Still, he continues, "In each friendly or conquered nation, Hitler must find a German population to give the whip to, or he must invent one."

43

Lupu says, "And they're all of a piece, your invented Germans. They're young, misfits, they're the angry and the bitter."

Malaparte is smiling. He is thinking now—aware of the colonel, the map behind him, purplish Germany overflowing its borders, spreading off the map itself, seeing the houses of the town through the window—of the stacks of rotting wood he saw set before houses. He thinks the people are wood poachers. They go into the countess's fields at night and gather the fallen branches. He thinks of babushkaed women going out in the night or in the mist and rain to poach wood. He thinks that the acne-faced boy is a poacher too, something furtive and sideways in his regard.

"Legally, Romania's independent, but all our products go to the Germans. Our oil's bought at their price. If we complain, Germany lets Hungary loose to take a bite out of us. Legally, I'm the police. But Jassy's a crossroads, and there's a permanent German intendance here of a hundred officers and men. And there's a German transit camp of regimental strength at the border twenty kilometers from here. Legally, I represent the king, but the Iron Guard Milice is sponsored by the king and receives money, arms, and instructions from the German SS. Once, to ward off German or Hungarian occupation, the king had the English option, the Russian one, and even the Italian one. Now it may be that to remain king he has only the one option of putting on the Iron Guard SS black uniform." He whispers, "Things are happening even now. Patriots and decent men are walking a tightrope." He pauses, embarrassed as if he has revealed too much, shown too much feeling. "What do you think, will the Russians hold?"

"In Russia, the Germans have taken a million prisoners and razed half the land. Here in Romania, your back's broken and they've never even stepped on you."
Lupu's voice is gray and official. "I must ask for all your papers."
"Do you want my money and my wristwatch too?"
"You've been an *enfant terrible* too long, Malaparte."
He has prepared a paper for Italian Captain Curzio Malaparte. He is restricted to the region of Jassy.
Malaparte leaves, thinking it is happening even now. He had thought they would, *noblesse oblige*, wait for him to arrive in Italy when Mussolini could again jail him. But no, it is now, or almost now. He has been, he has suspected, in their eye even since he left the front, he has been a fly in their eye since he came, journalist, guest, to look at their doings. He is thinking, good, there will be no more dinners where he will have to make jokes, he is smiling at the joke—What is the difference between a peasant and a poacher? only a landlord! There will be no more *enfant terrible*, no more prodigal son. He is tired of wearing uniforms and clothes that are not his. He is tired of waking everyday on dreams he will not permit himself to remember, of lying in bed worrying like an old man if the motor of his Ford will turn over. He will, poor nauseous old man, be locked away in a fortress tower. He will dress himself as a poet, an astronomer, and gentlewomen will come visit him in their finest silks and satins. They will curtsy for him, they will exchange ribbons and favors. He is walking in the narrow crowded labyrinth streets in the wake of a porter carrying a great bale of cotton on a platform on his back. The porter is bent almost horizontal to the street, the platform is attached to his forehead by a leather sling. Malaparte thinks, smiling, that there is so

much weight at the head that one does not feel the over-whelming weight on the back. He hears the cacophony of men hawking their wares, the hammering of brass, he smells the thick greasy smells. He wants to see into the small dark shops. He looks about at the faces of men, but they are blank masks hiding dark inner rooms. He feels a rising current in the street, a murmur of anger all about him. Poachers! he thinks smiling. Stealing blindly in the night, longing to take in the day! One cry rightly sounded and windows will pop open and women will pour their screams into the streets and men will explode in wild re-volt! Another porter passes, beast of burden whom he wants to think of as being able to defecate while walking.

These are the windowless backs of tall ghetto build-ings, looming wall of the ghetto. Inside are vast dark velvet-hung apartments, overflowing coffers, inside are the low cramped rooms of the thieving hunchbacked poor, inside are the narrow uneven corridors giving on rooms where women wear red.

In this new version of the story, he is witness only. The girl without a name whom he called Sarah. She fled the Germans into the forest, and she was flushed out with other girls, and some were sent away but she was touched and felt, pinched for firmness, and was recruited to serve the New Order in a brothel. The recruits were allowed to serve in the brothel thirty days. At the end of that time, they were replaced. "Do you think they will send us home?" she asked him.

He thinks of the girls who cannot sleep, whose bodies are covered with the touch of a thousand men. He sees the soft naked reclining body of the girl and it is frothed with the fantasies of men. He sees her sitting up in the cold night before morning, playing solitaire, and the red cards are success and health, but it is almost a new day, and each day is a year in her life, and all the last years of her life are only one day.

He shows his new paper to the Romanian guard at the ghetto gate. The guard lip reads what he can, it is enough for him to salute Malaparte in.

The crowded narrow ghetto streets are different from the Romanian market streets; here there are few porters, few moving carts, little of the contained violence of porter or cart drivers gesturing and crying men out of their way; here there is no hammering of metal. Here the energy and greasiness is in the voice and the eyes, in the thick lips of the Jews, and every Romanian stands straighter, and every peasant babushkaed Romanian woman is a Lady or a Madonna. Jews sidle up to Romanians and whisper into their ears, and they rub their thumb and forefinger together at the level of their eyes in gestures expressive of things long desired, vaguely soiled. The very air here is different, soiled. A Jew bumps into Malaparte, his twisted face smiles up at him and he whispers, "Do you want to buy gold? dollars?" "What shall I do with dollars?" Malaparte asks. "I've got U.S. dollars, Canada dollars. Or maybe you've got dollars to sell." The Jew's smile is of an intimate complicity; the Jew glances over his shoulder as if he were a marked man and thrives on that. Malaparte walks on. A Jew holds an overcoat under his nose. "Cashmere," the Jew says, but Malaparte can see it is not, and can see then that the Jew even knew he would know it was not. The Jew is caressing the material between thumb and forefinger. "Winter's coming, what will a gentleman do without a cashmere coat!" But Malaparte is lost then in memory seeing across the street two fuzzy-bearded students wearing long black caftans, big brimmed velvet hats, their earlocks

47

swinging. He thinks he hears a cart advancing over cobble-stones. All life has stopped. He turns, looking for the body cart. No. A small boy is looking up at him, speaking to him. "I beg your pardon," Malaparte murmurs and reaches into his pocket to give him something. And only then does he understand that the boy would sell him a packet of black market American cigarettes.

He stands before the display window of a fine Jewish delicatessen, the name *Boris Wienachtsman* printed in an arch over the door. He has always liked Jewish food, bas-tardized from all the nations of exile, synthesized within the laws of kosher, bled, smoked, fried, pickled. Here hang the dried hard salamis. They are a red lean beef spiced, he knows, with green garlic and black pepper pieces. There are the smoked herring, a tray of them, the crisp skins sparkling golden; there a slab of pink smoked salmon. The owner has arranged as if for children his products on green crepe paper as on grass, and these foods glow in the broad deep landscape; at the furthest reaches, like towers, stand bottles of dark wine and brandies.

Inside the store is the musk of smoked and dried things. There are barrels of olives and pickles in sour brine; there are barrels of cereals, herbs that even drying give off their flavor. A tall man in a shopkeeper's clean white coat comes to serve him.

Malaparte says, "I'm staying at the castle, what can I bring the countess?"

There is something familiar in the man's face, a manly squareness to his jaw, fine intelligent warm smile.

"I've been saving them for her, my last bottles of good scotch whiskey. The difference is the water used. These are made with pure spring water."

"Then she shall have them."

He enters deeper into the store as the shopkeeper wraps the bottles in newspaper. He looks across the long counter at shelves of canned goods. He has thought he has heard music. He looks into a long dark corridor.

"You're Malaparte, aren't you?" the shopkeeper asks.

The shopkeeper is facing him. This is neither attack or fawning.

"I've read you in Italian. I've never been as far as Capri, but I was in Venice."

Malaparte is touched that the man knows his places.

"For Venice, I named my son Marco."

Malaparte smiles. For Capri, I named my son The Goat. "For the Saint or the Piazza?"

The shopkeeper laughs. "For Marco Polo."

He feels a touch of impatience that he did not guess Marco Polo. He thinks of the grown man bending and kneeling to arrange the window display. You might have better named him Kublai Kahn. "You'd have been a traveler?"

He says so simply that Malaparte scorns himself for his impatience, "I'd have discovered all the pearls and riches of the world."

Malaparte indicates the barrels and shelves like glowing riches and says, "You've a trade that fits you like a glove."

"I've a trade, but diminishing stock," the shopkeeper replies. "I've no more coffee, no more tea."

I also have a trade, Malaparte thinks, and my stock too is diminishing.

The are standing in the dark shop, one almost as tall as the other, looking into each other's eyes, and Malaparte is liking this man, and again he hears music, a pianist repeating a phrase. They stand still, listening. Malaparte recognizes the longing Brahms even from the phrase that is now again stopped, echoing. Of course, he saw this man— loyalty written in his face, music in his fine lips—, a cello cradled between his thighs, held at his heart.

"Marco," the man calls into the dark corridor. "Boris Wienachtsman," the man now says, introducing himself. "This is my son Marco."

Malaparte wonders how this small soft pale boy can be this man's son. He inclines his head politely, but the young man cannot at first look him in the eye, and when he does there is an unnatural expanse of white in one eye, and then the pupil swoons up and away involuntarily. His hand, small and fine, does not grip Malaparte's; it touches his hand because it must, but even in that touch is the pull of withdrawal.

Malaparte is brought a chair. Tea is scraped up from a last tin; a tea kettle whistles; the tea is steeping. The father and son sit on crates. Malaparte is smiling to himself at the way the boy's hands hang loosely, the way the pupil swooned.

"In Venice, the cemetery is an island," Boris Wienachtsman says to his son as if that were wonderful.

"An on another island in the lagoon," Malaparte says, "Vivaldi, *Il Rosso,* taught the nuns to play the mandolin."

"Prato," Wienachtsman says to Malaparte, "you were born in Prato, in Tuscany."

Again Malaparte is surprised and touched. It is as if his places really existed.

"What is it like?"

"The country is lean. Every man is a hunter and poacher. There is a castle there too."

The merchant serves the tea dark in glasses. Sugar is found, *petits beurre,* halvah. They sip the tea amid the shadows, the smell of herbs, souring and smoked things. The light reflects golden, glowing, off the heaping surface of a barrel of wheat grain.

"Your name," the boy asks, his voice so soft that for an instant Malaparte wonders if he was addressed, "is really Sueckert?"

He has never liked that name, he does not like to hear it.

"Why did you choose Malaparte?" The boy goes on, the shyness and hesitancy of his manner somehow unpleasant.

"Should I have chosen Bonaparte?"

The merchant smiles, the young man looks away as if disappointed in the answer.

Malaparte asks, "Is it you who say that with Brahms all excitement is interior and a fantasy?"

The young man looks up, surprised.

"The thing with Brahms," Malaparte says, "is that he's too fat. Do you know the photographs of him where he's seated on a piano bench, that enormous belly and croup, the long hair and fat pudgy face. How can we take him seriously!"

"Yes," Marco says, "except for his beard, he even looks like a woman."

Malaparte laughs with surprise. "Do you play chess?" he asks the boy.

"My father does."

Malaparte knows the father's game, it is studied, regular. But playing the boy would be like playing on a board with a third dimension, attacks coming from beneath one's own pieces. He is looking at the father and son, and he understands now and is amused that the tall manly father is proud that the gnomelike son is even as he is.

"Did you go to school here?" Malaparte asks the boy.

51

"I've only been through high school."

"Marco wasn't well as a child," the father explains. "And, of course, we're not always welcome. There's been no way for him to continue to study music as he would."

"It's unimportant," the boy says, a shrug in his manner.

"In our world," the father says, "there's always been a *numerus clausus,* one Jew for a hundred Christians."

Outside, a horse and open carriage fill the narrow street, stopping it, blocking the light. The tall smooth-faced Inre of the castle, wearing dark livery, not bothering to descend from the driver's bench, rings his bell; the sound echoes up high between the facing ghetto buildings, and the horse restlessly pulls at its reigns and throws its head sideways, the big-toothed mouth slavering at the corner. Elena, dressed in black, her face sunburned dark, her dark hair tight to her head, sits high and immobile in the open carriage.

Marco goes into the street. He nods, almost a bow, to Elena who does not respond. He takes a list from the servant.

Malaparte is looking on from his chair in the dim interior, the sounds of the street entering the shop. Now the father is helping the son find and wrap the items, and Malaparte knows that the father and son have played music a hundred times in the castle. Elena—her lips pursed faintly in a small smile, the high cheekbones, the big eyes—looks on this cobblestoned ghetto street as if from a high balcony. The horse stamps its hooves. Once, it stretches the whole long side of its head almost to the display window, the big eye.

Marco carries a packed carton out to the driver. "Excuse me, *domna* Countess, there's no tea, there's no scotch whiskey."

"Find them," Elena says.

Marco, looking up at Elena, cocks his head as if against the sun.

Malaparte smiles at the merchant who waits uneasily. The tall servant looks to Elena and Elena nods at him. He removes his long whip from its stand-up place. Malaparte remembers his high-pitched voice. Still Marco does not move. Malaparte, studying, watching, waiting, thinks there is something in Marco ready to be beaten. He stands, guilty or not, but accepting, before Elena high in the carriage, and the tall dark-liveried servant, and the way he stands is yet a pride, like a knowledge whose price is that he be beaten.

The merchant's face is bloodless.

Malaparte offers the newspaper-wrapped bottles back to the merchant who takes them out into the narrow street where the servant has raised his whip.

6

Wearing the count's clothes, a silk foulard knotted loosely at his neck, Malaparte sits big, straight-backed, turning over cards at a small table in his high-ceilinged castle room.

The narrow leaded window he faces gives on the sloping field behind the castle, the looming shadowy forest. Darkness is falling, the mist rising like vapors. He thinks of the giant boar in the forest. He hears music in the castle, violin and piano. Tall, almost blind Axel Munthe is one of the dog-earred cards. Jacks are young princes, colonels. Queens are profounder cards, of spades—enveloping darkness, of diamonds—success. Kings are pompous villains.

Clubs, he thinks then, turning over the king of clubs, are the mist.

There is a knock at the servants' passage door in the paneling.

Marynona stands hesitant by the open door. "*Domnule* captain, the countess sent me that you're late."

Which countess, mother or daughter?

"Speak for yourself, Marynona."

She blushes.

He has approached her and his hands grip her arms even as she pulls back almost into the dark passage. Marynona, he will say later, you're as hairy as a goat.

"Don't you like me, Marynona? Don't you like me a little?"

He has always towered over women, he is a giant holding her to him, smiling at her a little as if he were a boy.

"*Domnule* captain," she says, breathing fast, shaking her head.

"Oh, don't *domnule* me!"

"The countess Elena—"

"Let the countess Elena go to the devil!" he says, his hand scooping under her skirt, finding its way into the moist hairy warmth. Her eyes are blurring, melting. And he brings his other hand from behind her, digging into the cleft between the cool cheeks, and his finger finds the tensed bud.

"No!" she moans, turning, twisting. "No!"

"Why not?" he coaxes, deepening his hold, gently forcing the bud, his finger popping then within. She is so roomy wet in front he almost forgets the finger there, she is tight behind, the ring tightening at the base of his big squirming finger. She is rising tiptoe off the floor, she is

54

perched heavily on his fingers, on his cupping hands, seventy cottony kilos, ten stone in soft globes. He is leaning his head over her shoulder to reach forward and back further into her. "Why not?" he insists as if he must know the reason.

Her dark face—her eyes swooning, the hot wild breath of her—is contorted with fright, her body is struggling within the parenthesis of his arms. "Why not?" he demands angrily. But even then she bursts his hold and twists out of his arms and is running away from him in the dim passage, her skirt brushing against walls. He will catch her and lay her on the stairs and ram the she-goat home, he will seat her like a doll spread-legged on the stairs, he will tumble her, face forward, and throw her skirt back over her head. He will play hide and seek with her outside all the bedrooms of the castle. He is smiling hard, racing up the winding stairs; he is reaching after her but the odor of her is so strong he thinks she is even yet on the tips of his fingers. So now, as he almost falls through a doorway after her into the big tower room, he, pursing his lips as if to whistle, hides his hands, clasping them, behind his back.

Everyone here turns to look, the slight smiles, Patrice seated at the piano, Rainer standing behind, each in his leather-belted and shining-booted uniform, gray-green Wehrmacht, black SS-like, Pauli and Elena in long gowns, red, black, dancing together. Malaparte glimpses the hand-filling ivory pieces of the chessboard, the greyhound stirring by the blazing fire. The countess is standing near a table of hors d'oeuvres at the wall; her as if carelessly combed shimmering hair halos her birdlike face, she wears a long dark velvet gown; she is looking on amused, distant, a tall whiskey glass in hand.

The music is only a waltz, three step simple thing. He

thought it was the dark minuet of the opening movement of the Brahms. He is troubled by something about the acne-faced boy at the piano; his hair is greased back on his head as who, whom he knew, wore his hair?

Pauli wears the same red shoulderless dress that wounds the tops of her small breasts. Her eyes are outlined green, her lips are painted bright red. She smiles briefly, moistly, at Malaparte, an intelligence like complicity in her eyes. She holds Elena at her hip and hand—he can almost feel the sharp lap bone of Elena in his hand—, long intertwining fingers, pointed red fingernails. He has thought Pauli, so tall, long, insectlike, and there is that in her strange abrupt grace. As for Elena, as darkly glowing as Pauli is brightly, she seems now unconscious of him, of the fair-haired German boy as of her son, she is smiling calmly as into a mirror into Pauli's face.

He crosses the flagstoned floor to the countess.

"We gather this way," she says as if mild apology, "for musical evenings."

He raises, bowing his head, her soft chinalike blue-veined hand to his lips, her fingernails glow a dull silver. There is no age to her.

Marynona stands waiting heavy and dull before them. She has the slumbering look of the people in the streets.

"Two fingers of scotch," he says to Marynona.

"Patrice," Elena calls as if peevishly to her son, "can't you play faster?"

The boy smiles over his shoulder; Malaparte sees for an instant the thick pores of his skin like the thick pores he remembers of the mother's skin. The boy hunches over the piano trying to build speed, and he looks, from the back, at the upright piano, intent, like a hunchback.

"Did he go to school here?" Malaparte asks about the boy, raising his voice for the music.

"He did," the countess replies, her voice trailing so that he know that he did not finish.

"He needs a father," Malaparte says and then tastes his whiskey. He smiles approvingly into the countess's eyes. "It's the pure spring water that makes the difference."

"Is it not?" the countess agrees.

The light from the blazing fire across the room glows red off the golden skin and dead eyes of the herring, smoked salmon sliced like pieces of muscled fat, gray caviar, each tiny pearl of it alive.

The herring has been soaked in cream, still there is a salty taste to it that enflames the lips and tongue. He spreads gray caviar on dark buttered bread, and it, on the enflamed flesh, soothes and irritates, even as then does the furry texture and the taste of the smoked salmon.

Rainer, standing cross-belted, booted, pale and alone, watches Elena dancing with Pauli. Malaparte thinks he himself has never been jealous of men but only of women.

"What's wrong, Curzio?" the countess asks.

"You should close the eyes of the herring."

She looks at the herring and then into his eyes.

"I think the boy should be whipped that he not turn out like me."

"What have you done now?" she asks, smiling faintly.

He does not answer. He is the hunchbacked boy with the slicked-back hair. Did Elena ask Patrice to comb his hair this way, the way he, in that time, did? He thinks she makes the boy into a hunchback; he thinks, What will the boy do in return? He wonders if it is not the countess who asked him to slick his hair back.

"Dance with me."

She smiles, We shall show them how to dance.

He bows his slicked-back-haired head to her. His big right hand presses her lightly at the velvet ribs behind her breast, her silver fingernailed hand presses his. He is, head held back, chest out, the fine hollow low in his back, a hero. They sweep across the vast polished floor of the Bruhl Palace, and they are sailing in the breeze, and all about them tall men and beautiful women are dancing, and somewhere is the president himself, and the military attachés who are all heroes and will be generals, and somewhere here a man's face is smiling nastily at him.

"Chess?" Pauli asks, almost as tall as he.

They are all standing about, smiling, challenging.

He sits in a low chair across from the red-gowned leg-spread Pauli.

"She's been studying moves all day," Elena says.

"Is it so important that you win?"

"I've no guardian angel," Pauli says.

"Where were you before you came here?" Malaparte asks, sensing the answer.

Pauli only smiles and studies the chessboard.

"She was visiting in Poland," Elena answers for her. "She was there even while you were."

There is something in Elena as sometimes in himself, a brooding slowness with words, the words held back by or dragging up other forces. He is studying the chessboard, but he cannot see it as the squares it is. It is a street map.

"Perhaps we met in Poland," Malaparte says, not allowing it to be a question.

Rainer says as if to praise Pauli's professionalism, "We played Ping-Pong to limber her body. What a player she is! 'Ja!' she says when she makes a point. 'Ja!' When she

58

makes a mistake, all her face turns into anger and she says
disgustedly to herself, 'Pauli, what's wrong with you!' "
Rainer's cheeks have colored a bit, there was a touch of
sarcasm in his voice.

"Do you know what I do when I make a mistake?"
Malaparte asks, looking up. The countess is crossing the
flagstoned room to leave, the halo of silver hair, a whisper
of velvet.

"You tell a story!" Pauli says.

"You visit Jews!" Elena says.

"All day long," he says, "I've studied Marx."

Elena smiles mockingly.

"Is Malaparte become a Marxist?" Rainer asks.

"Is Marx become a harpist?" Malaparte replies.

"Is Marx become an angel?" Rainer asks, pleased with
himself, daring the famous Italian.

"All Jews are angels," Malaparte agrees.

"There are not enough trees in Jassy," Patrice, his hair
greased back, says, putting his hand to his throat, "to
make angels of them all."

Malaparte looks into the acne-faced boy's eyes, and the
boy is looking through a transom at him and his mother.

Malaparte says softly, "I'm a Harpo Marxist."

Patrice says, "You're a nothing Marxist!"

"Harpo Marx is a prophet," Malaparte says and smiles
the way he does when he is about to tell a story. But there
is no story, he is thinking of an astronomer, an astrologer.

"He is a prophet bird," Patrice says. "Cheep! Cheep!"

There is such malevolence and triumph in the boy,
there is such mocking anticipation in the mother, that he
knows he will lose.

The German lieutenant, blond messenger god beautiful, is pale and alone again. He has sat down at the upright

59

piano and is meditatively picking out the barest music, bird in a forest, music with no end. Malaparte cannot concentrate on the game. Beneath the squares he sees still the lines of the street map. He is wandering in the labyrinth lanes of the map. He moves his bishop to threaten Pauli's king's bishop's pawn. "Ja! Ja!" she exclaims and brings her queen into his king's corner. He smiles into the mocking faces and he feels there is a large florid face above smiling on. He thinks the ceiling is the guardian angel giant face of the German governor-general of Poland, Reichsfuehrer Frank.

Rainer is repeating the same bird in a forest music, long pauses, long moments of sinking flight. It is the most mysterious music Malaparte has ever heard. It is like walking in the dark forest. It is like being part of the forest, like being an eye there looking on, and then again, the bird flies, like my own breathing, lifting, gliding, long sinking.

He knows he must attack her queen at every move. If she has the chance to bring even a second piece into the attack, he will be lost. He has allowed himself to lose a corner pawn, but only in order to vector an attack. "Ja! Ja!" He did not see. She sweeps center to, taking a second pawn, put his king in check. He is condemned to a slow losing counting game of exchanges.

"I resign," he says grandly, standing, spreading his arms.

"You're a coward," Pauli says. "The game isn't over."

"Were you a man, I'd challenge you to a duel." Still, he sits down again and resumes the game.

Pauli is smiling. "You were a hero, but you've become self-indulgent. Even your horse is turned inwards."

Each square of the board is a trap. Her pieces seem to surge from off the board. They are forest knights come from behind thick trees. The furry salty taste of smoked things makes him lick his lips.

He is, in a deep armchair, facing the blazing fire, the logs crossed within radiant, a mass beneath the crux of the logs of glowing debris, embers like pearls, small white gases, a nimbus yet glowing behind, drawing within; the flames above the logs are like veils, licking and moist. The greyhound, the tight rib cage pressed to the stone floor, lies primly facing the fire, ever alert. Malaparte is drinking scotch. The German is at the piano, he has opened the collar of his tunic. The tall women are dancing together. Behind the music of the piano is the string and piano music of the night before, and behind that is that of a too-lipsticked girl hammering at a run-down piano.

'Malaparte,' an open-tunicked German officer asks, 'why don't you sing "Deutschland uber alles" with us?'

'I'm an Italian.'

'Of everyone in the world, Italians are just below Germans.'

'That's what I've always been afraid of.'

They laugh, they slap him on the back.

Why do you want to kill Jews? he will ask the boy.

"Tell me the story of the astronomer," Elena asks, kneeling by his chair, her slender-fingered cool hand on his, she jealousying now Pauli as the German before, jealousying her very dog.

"Did I mention him?"

"You spoke of a man who pasted stars on rags that he wrapped about himself."

"He sold fortunes," he says, remembering.

The women are dancing, tall, ghostlike in each other's long arms, and the lieutenant is drunk on the music, playing the piano in such a way that one knows what he is feeling. It is Brahms or Schubert, it is that abstraction of pain that is beauty, mastery of pain, molding of it, timelessness of pain. Patrice would, to this slow singing music, dance with his mother, but, cutting in, he hesitates and then asks Pauli. Pauli is so tall over him, and yet he presses himself lewdly to her, and Pauli is smiling and almost laughing up at the ceiling, and Elena is glaring at Pauli.

If you kill Jews now, what will you do when you grow up?

I will fuck them, like you.

He is lost in the castle searching for its center. Come, Marynona, I smell you here, I smell you there, I smell those Frenchies everywhere. He is in the passage outside the countess's door, a candle in hand. He is smiling, standing hunched in the count's tweed jacket and silk foulard, he will worship at the eye.

"It's the last of the whiskey," the countess says.

She is standing high on a ladder, a palette that rides up one side of the ladder is fixed near her breast; she wears a painter's smock; candelabra are on the floor in the center of the room, her own whiskey glass, the nearly empty bottle; her hair halos high against and as if out of a peacock blue and green in a painted wall. She leans against the ladder to reach her fine paint brush high into the wall. Malaparte, sipping his drink, standing by the ladder, sees below the reaching arch of her small foot a dark pond in the painted wall, goldfish glowing darkly within; he sees ladies in high-bodiced dresses and conical hats walking on pebbly lanes primly in the night as if it were day. He sees an owl perched high on a tree branch; everywhere are almond-shaped leaves crenelated razor-sharp, eyes of the night.

"You too would be a magician," he says.

She does not hear the scorn and anger and smiles down at him from the eyes of the garden. "What I'd like is that what I live in the day, I undo here at night."

"I'd have pajamas," he says. "I'd have a dressing robe and slippers." He reaches up and takes her hand in his.

"This isn't what you want," she says, pale. "You want Marynona," she says, teasing, hurt that he does. "You want nothing that I can give." Her hand is pulling from his, or is it pulling him up the ladder. He wants to take his place over her. She is looking down at him and is shaking her head at the fascination she sees in his eyes. "Call Inre, please."

He smiles.

"He's never far," she says.

"Is he? Inre!"

There are steps outside a door.

"The Tartars," Malaparte says in her tower room to Elena, embers still glowing in the fireplace, he sitting in the deep armchair where he sat before, "tie the living to the dead. They knot the thighs and waists of their German prisoners to those of their own dead. They knot them together at the neck so that face is to face. And the living warm the dead until the dead begin to smile and stiffen and move, and the dead, you know, have no shame and nothing to lose."

The tall slender woman in black has knelt between his thighs and she says, smiling to his smile, "*Je jouis mieux toute seule.*"

"Is it not so?" he responds sadly. She opens his clothes and reaches her long fingers within. He reaches his hand to her high cheekboned face.

She snaps her teeth at his fingers, the greyhound stirs by the fire. She says, smiling, "Don't tickle the lion."

Now her hand brings the bird out into the open. It is tender, it twitches and rises as her fingertips raise it to her lips.

His thick massive thighs spread wider. Her lips blow teasingly on the tautening flesh. Her tongue teases the eye of him. Her mouth embraces the length of it, possessing it sideways, each open-mouthed kiss a seal and tattoo on it. Now she touches the head of it with little kisses, and her mouth sucks him in, and he has entered the circling, enfolding warm wet cavern, and all his other body is lax, he curled back in himself a hundred thousand years before, though then he feels, laughing menacing reminder, the polished wet smoothness of ivory. Her eyelids are drooped, she rides the still rising instrument forward and back, taking him from the lips deep, deeper. And even then he feels the long fingers of her sliding under his thighs to the cleft of him, and a single long finger rides onto his anus. It is only an accident, he feels her teeth laughing at his member. He is within, walls gliding on him, tongue wetly tightening spaces. He is above it all, looking down at it all, what is happening below is not of him. He is reaching within her, the blind eye of him searching for the dim chamber of her lidded eyes.

He is searching in the castle still. Here a door is ajar. In the dark room, Pauli says, "Come."

He enters the bed. Her long back is to him. He puts his hand low to her, and her hand is already there, fingernails sharply pointing the way. She folds herself to her knees, camel crouching, and she spreads her legs that he take her from behind. His hand, directing his member, touches again her long sharp fingers between thighs and cheeks, and she is moist at the small spot, and her fingers prick his member into her. He enters tightly, the moist muscles play on him, and he is croup-riding her up and down, and he has never been held so well, and she is tossing and swaying him, and he would reach down the front of her body to her Venus' mount and Venus' eye, but his hand strives against hers, and suddenly he is holding a small stiff infantile finger there and a small sack like a cloven thing.

It is dawn. Someone is kissing him on the cheek. Get away, filth! He is rising to his knees on the small cobblestones in the castle courtyard. It is only a dog. It is Prince. He looks into Prince's loyal face. The dog is striated with festering whip marks.

He does not know where he has been, in which room last. He stood staring at the bicephalus in its niche, one lidded eye of each head lower than the other. He remembers now the man-woman's laughter, and from time before he hears the laughing giant florid-faced one telling him, "I shall show you what no man has ever seen. Are you man enough for that?" He is invisible. He is invisible stepping into the mist.

Two:

Forbidden Cities

1

Malaparte is billeted in a small stone cabin, gatehouse at the entry of a broken-walled orchard at an outskirt of Jassy. One wall of the cabin is built up from the orchard wall, and the window there gives on, some distance away, a white birch tree lined road.

Prince lies sick in shadows in a corner of the cabin; sometimes he raises his head, and open mouthed, pants for breath; sometimes he paws weakly the wood plank floor to cover his excrement. In the center of the cabin is a small now cold wood-burning stove with rusted flue pipes that rise through the roof; on the floor is a windup record player with some records. There is a thin mattress on the floor by a wall.

Malaparte wears the sky blue Italian army uniform. But he has not shaven and there is a black gray stubble on his face. He must go out and buy alcohol to wash Prince's festering wounds, he must buy a lamp, food, more drink. He wants permission to buy gasoline for his Ford parked outside by the well. But has he not already gone out with the same intention yesterday or the day before? Has he not already been to see Colonel Lupu? 'What do you need gasoline for, Malaparte? You've been restricted to the town, you can go nowhere. Or do you too want to start fires in Jassy? There are partisans in the forest, terrorists.' What else did he say that he cannot now remember?

"Be good, Prince." Flies are buzzing over the dog.

He is at the door, but he has forgotten something. He sees himself looking through his bag, throwing clothes this way and that. What has he lost or misplaced that is so important? Only the cards? The camera! He hangs the small camera by its strap from his shoulder.

He is approaching Jassy, these narrow streets of wood plank house after wood plank house, and chickens pecking into the black dirt. He is looking at a rain barrel. He springs the lid of the camera open, the lens riding forward, pulling small bellows out. It is a Certo Dolina, Italian fabrication, but the lens eye is German. He raises the camera to his eye and focuses the lens in on the scummy surface of the stagnant water in the rain barrel. Still, he does not snap the picture. It is as if he is only framing what he sees, impressing something, by delimiting it, on his mind. He has a thousand such framed and stopped impressions, and, even as he frames what he now sees, something else appears. He is playing chess. The tall white-coated shopkeeper is seated hunched on a crate opposite him.

"What do you want here?" the son, Marco, asks.

The father says, "Let him alone, it's not his fault."

"What's not my fault?"

"Why do you keep coming back here?" Marco insists.

"I've always liked Jews," Malaparte answers. "I've always been drawn to Jews. There's something womanlike in Jews, the way some of you curl your hair at your ears, the softness of your hands. The way, when I'm even falling to pieces, I can beat you at chess."

"You come to watch us, to spy on us."

He hears a hammering on metal. Shoemakers, copperworkers, are bent over themselves in front of their closetlike shops. He must buy a lamp. All about him in these crisscrossing twisting streets are the poor, their faces thick-featured, the slumbering look of beasts. They jostle him, they rub against him. He hears a rising thundering clattering and turns and presses himself to a wall as a teeth-clenched horse races a flat wagon, the bald driver standing and whipping the horse, down the narrow cobblestoned street.

He enters the store and no one is there. He whistles a tune, he puts his hand into a barrel of golden cereal and lets the cereal fall back like sand between his fingers. He hears a sound of a piano and he saunters back into the rooms behind the store. In a study lined with books, the boy is seated at a piano, his small hands close to his bent body like movement stopped, paralyzed.

"You come to the ghetto to look at yourself looking at us."

He has salami, herring, black bread, bottles. He has a hammered copper lamp. He has forgotten alcohol for the lamp. No matter, he will use brandy. There is a book in his side pocket. He is looking at a wall of books. Books lean one on the other, scores on each shelf, unevenly cut pages pressed together. He reads a word of a title, *Civilization*. He has dreamed of books falling like a stone wall crumbling, pages opening, faces, languages he does not know. He has dreamed of his books, and there is always one more than he has written. Is it this book? The book in his pocket is thin. *The Communist Manifesto*. Is that all? Couldn't he have stolen better? He tosses the book onto his mattress on the floor. He goes out again leaving the door open that Prince follow him into the orchard if he like, but, once in the orchard, he remembers that Prince was lying in his corner breathing like whining.

He has come out into the evening freshness with a drink in hand, he will stroll his Roman emperor busted garden lanes before dinner. He knows these bud-eyed villains; hang togas across our shoulders, curl our hair forward, and we are even they. But here biting gnats are rising and buzzing at his face, and these trees—he walking down the length of the orchard, the light of the setting sun bleeding into one side of the trees—have grown wild, and thorny bramble grows between them and about their trunks. His booted foot hits into a stone and he stumbles forward. His hands are scratched, he waves gnats from his eyes, he slaps at his chin, his cheek. He looks at the stone that projects from the ground. There are carvings on it. He thinks there are other such stones hidden in the bramble here. He picks up a stick charred like the smooth scales of a snake. He must gather wood, the night will be cold. Distantly, through the crumbled further wall of the orchard, he sees high flaming camp fires. He steps through the wall; he stands tall in the flat abandoned field, and he turns then hearing from the birch tree lined road the sounds of horses and carriages, bells ringing.

These are the fast two-wheel one-horse carriages of the top-hatted rich. It is a line of elegant carriages—the tops drawn back like open umbrellas to catch the wind—silhouetted against the last bleeding red of the day, flickering like an off-timed film between the regularly spaced birch trees.

He crosses fields slowly, his hand reaches to his collar as if for the cold, as if the collar were that of a greatcoat.

Gypsy wagons are parked in a circle enclosing the

camp fires. They are long and heavy, their tops are curved outward like sailing schooners. They are painted blue and red, but the paints have faded and are washed like the pastels of clouds. There are bells attached to the schooner corners that sound weakly in the breeze. The gypsy horses are tied to stakes in the open, they are heavy-footed big-bellied beasts.

Malaparte stands tall, his hand at his collar, in the shadow of a schooner wagon. The stout nobles and notables of Jassy sit on rugs cross-legged like pashas. They have brought ice buckets with champagne, and they serve each other from the frothing long-necked bottles. They open their plump hands to gold-toothed bent gypsy women who come among them to read their fortunes in their soft palms beneath their gold wedding bands. They promise them success, long life, adventure. Gypsy men play guitars, something in their swarthy earringed faces of beggars and thieves. A gypsy sings a plaint, it rises from the belly; the gypsy bends over himself to retch up from himself the deepest sounds we know. And even as he finishes, dark young gypsy women saunter among the nobles and notables, jingling their firelight-gleaming necklaces, bracelets, and anklets.

The bitter smile has not left Malaparte's face. The rich and how they live, the name he hates. Is that all? But he sees then, standing in shadows even as he, watching the gypsies, two tall slender boys in gray greatcoats. And then he sees, the light glowing at her large eyes and high cheekbones, that one slender boy is Elena—her hand softly pressing her coat collar to her throat—, and the other is the taller Pauli, and even then he sees that they are coolly, absently, holding hands, a smiling attentiveness in them to the night and all they see. Malaparte does not know where the trouble in him comes from, he is short of breath. He is walking now across abandoned smoke-misted fields. There are smouldering fires everywhere, the smell of sulfur is in the air, and the ground is thick with ash, every step raising it, and other greatcoated ghosts walk in the ash, and then he sees looking up agonizedly at him the twisting big-eyed head of a horse.

He cannot sleep. Outside, the mist is rising from the earth, sounds come from outside like a sighing breathing. He has stuffed newspaper in the cracks between the window frames, but the mist seeps into the cabin. There is an odor here. He must sleep. It is days since he has slept. He lies back, he closes his eyes, he is on the brink of sleep, and suddenly he pulls back as if his foot is really at the edge of a pit. He closes his eyes and the dark about him is the dark of closed eyes, but he begins to think that his eyes are open and he is short of breath and he opens his eyes for light and reference, but it is the perfect dark that surrounds him, and he is sitting up suffocating, gasping. The lamp *is* lit, there is a fire in the stove. The book clutched in his hand is reference. It is all the fault of capital!

What's the syndrome, doctor? When I close my eyes, I'm not afraid. The fear comes only when, eyes closed, I think that when I open my eyes it will be as if they were closed.

And the suffocation?

The suffocation comes *before* I open my eyes.

Are you afraid of death?

I'm afraid of falling, of the perfect dark.

Then you've only to keep your feet on the ground and keep your lamp lit.

Malaparte bends to Prince in a dim corner. The odor

rises thick about him. He caresses the dog's thick neck, the skin of the dog is matted, sick. In the night, there are no flies. He has not changed his water, there is a thin scum over it.

He drinks from the bottle. He reads: "Modern bourgeois society with its relations of production, of exchange, and of property, a society that has conjured up such gigantic means of production and exchange, is like the sorcerer who is no longer able to control the netherworld whom he has called up by his spells." He winds up the phonograph. He sees himself searching in the dark in the orchard, he sees chickens floodlighted in the night pecking into the black earth. He puts the needle on a record. It is "Until Tomorrow," sung by a man, his voice sweet and husky. He lies on the mattress on the plank floor. Until tomorrow, he sings along, Marynona. He will let his eyes close little by little. He is crossing the mist in a greatcoat, boots, his visored cap. But now the record is ended and the needle is grating softly and, even as that sound dies, he hears a train far off in the night and again he is sitting up, suffocating, gasping for breath. But again there is light, it is the lamplight that smells so rotten sweet, brandy. He is looking at the small stove, the crack of white light in the vent of the small door of it. The flames are drawing, the stove is breathing.

He is lighting his way with a flashlight outside in the orchard gathering wood for the stove. Wood, fallen from the fruit trees, is hollow, light almost as paper. It is infested perhaps with ants and worms, but it does not matter, it is night, they are still, they will spit and sputter in the fire. He finds vinelike knotted wood; his hands strain to break the wood small enough for the stove. He will break a spearlike branch from a dead shrub. He grips the branch and is pricked by juniper needles that stun his hands like a poison. He stumbles again on a stone. These are pairs of *s*'s coiled snakelike on each other framing a swastika. He is smiling. It is a wheel, it is turning. He is following a chicken in the dark, poaching. He is about to swing his arm and catch a stick leg of it, but it jumps the crumbled wall, and he, following after, is suddenly taken hold of, and greatcoated Elena and Pauli are pushing him to the ground, stilling him. "Not a word! If they see you," Pauli whispers, smiling, "it's your life!"

He is lying on the ground between their trousered legs, tented by their greatcoats, the woolly warmth like a cloud over him. It is surely a game, a hide and seek, they are full of secrets and excitement. He looks from the ground up a great distance of greatcoat, and Pauli, he sees, is holding a camera to her eye. He too would frame what he sees. He bends his fingers into a frame before his eyes. He sees torches, he hears a loud wailing sound. Twenty shawled old women, each carrying a flaming torch, wailing as they walk, peering into the darkness, are approaching. Behind them, he sees the white-shifted almost naked forms of young women; barefoot, their hair down, they sweep scythes before them. The old women are bent and in black, and they are shaking small sticks white like bones at shadows, and sometimes one of the lithe young women in white—the flames bloodying their shifts, their bare arms— swings her scythe violently as if to cut a swathe in something that is not there, and then the dark old women turn and, shouting, stamping their feet, shake their bones as if at the spirit the girl has cut down.

"Cover your face!" Pauli whispers urgently. Because old women, their haggish faces lit by torches, are widening from the line of procession to approach and peer and scowl at the tall slender greatcoated figures. And only now does Malaparte see that, even as the old women precede, the young are cutting a swathe for and are a shield before a laboring woman, heavy, leaned forward, pulling, it seems a second woman. The first woman is dark with labor and sweat, and he sees that she is harnessed to and pulling through the earth a plough that the second woman keeps pointed into the earth. Pauli and Elena, Malaparte glimpses from below, have removed their caps and let fall their flowing hair, and Pauli has stretched her arms as if to say, Here I am, you see all of me!

They are gone now, the slender greatcoated figures following the procession. Where the earth was ploughed, the mist is rising thick.

He is kneeling, looking to the small door of the dying breathing stove. He has been kneeling here staring into the door—hours, days, paralyzed.

2

Everywhere about me is rising mist. I approach the two visor-capped greatcoated officers.

"You're late, Malaparte!"

He is my guide, my teacher, my guardian angel, great florid faced German Governor-General Frank, Reichsfuehrer of Poland. I have seen him wearing a fur coat draped over his shoulders, and then he seemed like one of those dark heavy birds that must run to lift off. Still, he is blond and blue-eyed, clear-eyed, something radiant and almost beautiful about him, a confidence, a solidity of stout flesh and small white teeth.

He appears in my life the first time not a year ago,

preceded by backward glancing, forward rushing lean aides, and followed by others, black and gray uniformed, silver braided, masked by their own self-importance as by their obsequious subservience, he too masked, but his mask indivisible, an inscrutable smile. They come in a swarm across the marble floor of the Bruhl Palace toward his offices where I and others are waiting. He stops in front of a group of uniformed school children. A boy is pushed forward to present him with a bouquet of flowers. But the boy is nervous and the welcoming speech does not come to his lips. Frank leans forward and puts his hand on the boy's shoulder and it is like a benediction, and the boy recites. Frank chooses now to look me up and down—I am a head taller than he, I am wearing a fresh uniform, polished boots, my visored cap is pressed to my side under my arm—and to recognize me.

"I've always heard that your head was like a bullet. Are you, Malaparte, Mussolini's secret weapon?"

His crowding aides, who were touched, as masks can be touched, when he set the boy at ease, now laugh as masks can laugh.

I bow my head and shoulders so that the bullet is pointed at him and I cry, "Ready! Aim! Fire!"

There is no laughter. He is called the Deutsches Konig vom Poland, it is said he would be King of all the East— Hungary, Romania, Bulgaria, Russia. He can have me birched like a schoolchild, he can have me arrested, he can have me shot. Mussolini would congratulate him. But no, now he begins to laugh, and now all his generals and colonels are laughing.

He takes my arm and leads me into his vast office. He speaks flawless Italian to me. He studied architecture in Florence. He aspirates like a Florentine. We talk, sit, and stroll in the dimly lit marble-floored office as if it were the tower and sculpture-shadowed Piazza Signoria. He raises the question of Michelangelo versus Donatello, the external versus the interior; he speaks of schools, of manner. I reply that they are temperaments, not schools. He smiles serenely. He says his ideal is even mine.

"What ideal?"

"That men be better! That men be more! It's you who wrote, 'There is no Thou Shalt and Thou Shalt Not. The only shalt a man knows is I shalt, is I shalt discover the force of me, the sources of force, and I shalt know how to use them. We shalt destroy the weak and corrupt that oppress us, we shalt struggle against every established order and morality until we uncover in the ashes the eternal one.' You said everything there, except what we're now on the brink of—the New Order. It's not for nothing that our Fuehrer loves architects above all men." He sees my smile. "Your recent reportages have angered Himmler. Beware the SS," he whispers as if suggesting they could be listening here even now. "*I* understand irony, but irony must never get in the way of vision. Temperament, Malaparte, *becomes* school, and one musn't be moody. So! What can I do for you?"

"*Carte blanche.*"

He laughs, delighted. "At least tell me for what."

"That I can go anywhere, that I be allowed in all the forbidden cities of Poland."

"It is yours!" he says and holds out his hand. Every nail is finely manicured. His hand is, in appearance as in touch, fine, beautiful, and cool. He says, holding my hand, "I'll give you the permissions you need, the introductions, but you'll not write anything until you've seen it all, you'll not begin to judge until you've heard all the witnesses."

"Malaparte," Governor General Frank calls out one evening some weeks later across the long banquet table, the wine-glowing shining faces of generals and governors, of their stout wives, "have you been to the ghetto?" He knows I have. I had to pass through a guarded entry. I was given a brochure, a map. "How did you find the Jews?" "Dirty."

Everyone in the vast echoing palace hall laughs. My German itself sounds *schmutzig.*

"They cannot be blamed," blonde bare-shouldered Frau Frank says. "The Jews have no soap."

"They'll soon have no excuse," Frank says. "Our scientists have discovered a new way to make soap. It costs next to nothing. It is made of a substance that is as abundant as we want it to be. The Jews will wash."

"What is it made of?" I ask.

"Soaps are made of fats, oils, ashes. What do you want it to be made of?"

I pale as he stares into my eyes.

"Yes, Malaparte, it is a soap made of—shit!"

"Of shit," I repeat, pensive, uneasy.

"Of shit. So you see," Frank says, a silence now at the table as all attention is forced by his clear blue-eyed look to me, "in the future you needn't walk through the streets of the ghetto whispering, 'I beg your pardon.' "

They are looking at me as if I am a silly child.

"The children," I observe coolly, "are skeletal."

"Like their parents," Frank says nodding, "they are mournful. But German children smile and are confident. Why don't you visit the German children of Poland who are going now to German schools and learning German culture?"

"How can Jewish children smile?" I ask. "They've no

games but to skip after the body wagons as they go from building to building filling up with their dead."

"They are like rats following the dead," Frank says. "They are like angels without wings."

"Do you want us then to give them wings?" Frank says, and he waves his arms as if they are wings and we are all laughing.

But later, Frank grows silent and leaves the table. Everyone acts as if it is nothing, and then, distantly, we hear piano music of Chopin. For an instant, I think it is the ghost of Paderewski playing in the same grand reception hall of this palace where I heard him twenty years before. I think I am twenty years younger, prouder, and that about me are the lean eagle-faced counts of Poland, the pale slender women. But then I see the firm red cheeks of the black and gray uniformed men, the button eyes welling sentimental, and I see that the bare-shouldered stout fraus have real tears at their eyes, and only then do I remember Frank's hands, the fine beauty, strength and coolness of them.

"When he's overburdened," Frau Frank whispers to me as if it were my fault, "he retires to his aerie and plays Chopin."

"Every king must have his tower."

"You've hurt him," she sxplains. "Apologize. Can't you see—listen!—how he loves humanity!"

"If only they knew!"

I enter the dim hall and watch him playing. He is alone, he does not know he is observed. And he does love humanity. He is one of those who plays with the back straight, with the head looking up as if he would always be in touch with his inspiration. And the music is beautiful. He finishes and, seeing me, smiles like a man awakening,

and for what can I apologize when all is new? He is im-
bued with a radiant sadness. "Malaparte," he says, "do
you know what I can't understand? When Chopin was
sick, he stayed a winter in a monastery in Majorca. It was
one of the great creative moments of his life. I've visited
the monastery, I've played on the piano he composed at.
It's a long drafty gallery. It's a small upright, its sound is
tinny, there are broken keys that only thump. Can you see
him there, playing, composing, cold, coughing? Malaparte, must beauty always come from suffering?"

The greatcoated man waiting for me in the mist with
Governor-General Frank is a colonel. This is a man who
does not sleep well, one sees it in his mournfulness. First, I
thought he was mournful as a colonel is mournful when his
career has nowhere to go. And then I recognized, like
looking into a forgotten mirror image, that he has been a
prisoner, that, locked away from everyone, cramped between four walls, with only the bare cot and stinking toilet,
with no mirror, he has looked deeply into his soul and it has
made a lasting impression. He is, Frank has told me, a
brave man. He stood up in the last war to the Turks who,
screaming, charged in waves with bayonets. After the war
he wanted, like us all, more, other, and he joined secret
organizations. When Hitler came to power, he was—for
the years he had spent a patriot in prison—made a guard in
one of the first concentration camps, and then he rose to be
a commander. He is commander now of Auschwitz-
Birkenau, and is, Frank joked, properly mournful, reign-
ing as he does over the dead.

"We've removed," Frank says, "an alien body from
the nation, a parasite, a disease. Fixed on the Aryan body,
the Jew grew strong. Sucking the life out of the Aryan, he
corrupted him. We've become physicians of the nation's

body, we've done as physicians do in the case of an epidemic: quarantine, sterilize, cauterize. And what we've done for ourselves, we're doing now for Europe. And all of Europe is thanking us."

"We treat Seven Day Adventists the same as Jews," the camp commandant says. "But I assure you, when you deal with men who believe as firmly in their principles as do the Adventists, who have such dignity in their misfortune, the task becomes harder. The Jews are corruption itself. With their arrival in the camp came bribery, homosexuality."

Auschwitz by Night.

Tableau Number One:

I stand with my guides at spy windows like camera lenses in a wall. I was not allowed to bring my Certo Dolina. I am my camera. I have not felt before, why should I feel now? Distance. We are in the world of the dead. Everything is camera-lens upside down, there is no substance here. Inside a brightly lit room, three women are waiting, each at a cot. They wear the striped dresses of prisoners, socks, wooden-soled shoes. They wear the green badge triangle of common law prisoners, the red one of prostitutes. Unlike other women prisoners, their hair has not been cut. They are coarse-faced, their bodies have never been theirs. Now, three men are brought into the room. They wear on their striped pajamalike uniforms the pink badge triangle of the homosexual.

"We've given them outdoor work to make them feel like men," Frank says. "Now, if they go at it directly, there's hope for their release."

The prostitutes lie back and raise their skirts. One spits on her fingers to moisten herself between her legs. One of the shaven-headed homosexuals, a strong-bodied smiling blunt-faced man, is immediately in position.

Frank says, speaking of a young man who stands hesitant like a boy, "What do you think, Malaparte, will he be sick? Were you ever sick?"

"Never!" I answer from my spying crouch. "I've never been sick!" And I feel then a warmth in my crotch, proof even of desire.

We watch, eye to the lens, and the strong-bodied man and his prostitute are rising and falling, and the young man's prostitute is trying with her hand to stiffen him to fit him in, and though the young man is lying on her, he cannot look her in the face. The third homosexual is an older man, his gestures so effeminate that the woman, even before he lies on her, looks at him with scorn. Now he is sitting up on the cot, his shaven head in his hands.

Tableau Number Two:

Greatcoated, we enter a barrack. We stand by the door. This is not one of the crowded sleeping barracks, a thousand men cramped to each other in five-tiered bunks. No, this barrack is clean, disinfected, and everything here is stilled, cottony, twenty men standing in a line. They are not aware of us except as a snail might be aware of a giant, and we are focusing down on them, watching here something mysterious, I do not know what. They hold up their pajamalike pants, for they have no belts, no string. Their eyes seem large, perhaps because their cheeks are sunken, or for the relatively limited movement of the eyelid and the pupils. Each of them must, when it is his turn, step up to a waist-high metal counter and answer questions. I realize now that each time a prisoner steps up to the counter, the electric lights dim.

"We give serious consideration to all solutions," Frank says in a stage aside. "One is that we make the Jew into a race of—mules."

"Do they know?" I ask behind my hand.

The mournful camp commandant answers, "Many develop burns at their thighs and genitals."

Tableau Number Three:

There are strangely glowing lamps here. On shelves are a hundred skulls, each labeled. The long white-coated professor shows us typical skulls of Jews. He explains the ecto- and endomorphic psychology of Jews. I do not ask if he chooses the skulls randomly or preselects them. Each bone has been measured and cross-measured, the cranial capacity calculated. There are ledgers open on tables, meticulous entries have been made. He shows me two skulls and asks which is the Jewish one. I choose the one with the bullet hole. He laughs. "That one," he says, "is ten thousand years old. They drilled a hole in the head and sucked out the soul."

But my attention is on the lamplight, the glow resembles something I know.

The professor is smiling at my interest. "We've isolated prisoners with tattoos," he says, something more intense even than the interest of science in his eyes.

I touch the lamp shade. A perspiration comes off on my fingertips that is not from my own skin.

Tableau Number Four:

We are at a train station. It is night, lean dogs are barking, a train is arriving, a pajama-uniformed orchestra strikes up a Viennese waltz.

The men and women pouring down out of the cattlecars still have hats, overcoats, baggage. They still have hair, exotic in this place. There are children and infants among them.

SS in black separate the healthy from the sick, the aged and infants from the able-bodied. Mothers must remain with their infants. Here they have caught a mother who has abandoned her child. "Jewish mother! Unnatural thing!" An SS calls and beats her with his truncheon to the ground where the dogs crowd about her, snapping.

Tableau Number Five:

The shower room is vast, it is cement buried in the ground. There are a hundred shower spigots attached to the walls. The Jews, naked, are filling the shower room. Mothers hold the hands of their young children. Some mothers, holding the hands of their children, would be modest yet and they hunch their shoulders forward to hide their breasts. Some women keep their hands crossed over their sex. Children are uneasy, they can feel their mother's fear through the touch of her hand.

Now the shower room door is shut tight behind them. Five hundred men, women, and children look to the door. Their frightened eyes race then over the walls of the room searching for a way out; they stare at the tiny holes in the shower spigots, at the high blind glass of our spy windows, at the metal latticed air ducts at the base of the walls. One woman begins to scream. Of course, we, behind our spy windows, cannot hear. Immediately, many men and women are screaming. We see, as one can see only in a painting or a photograph—the absence of sound, the distance, permitting us to discover—all the tensed muscles of the scream, the bulging-veined lengthening of the throat, the projection of the jaw. Those near the airtight door begin to pound on it, but hundreds now push toward the door and those who are against it are pressed flat there, their faces turned up for air, their arms spread high.

The gas-masked specialists on the roof shoulder-high above the ground—we must bend almost in half to keep our eye to the spy windows—release from long metal tubes sparkling crystals into the central air ducts. The crystals accumulate at the air duct openings at the base of the shower room walls and, with the contact with air, produce the gas. The gas is already seeping into the crowded shower room. Now all there is writhing movement and open-mouthed screams of naked reaching bodies. The gas spreads and rises in a mist, veiling first feet and knees, rising on the bodies of children, vapors curling higher. They are coughing now, they are screaming, some cup their noses and mouths with their hands. They are pushing and tearing at each other to be as far from the poison as they can, they are stepping on others to escape the rising poison. They are reaching to the shower spigots to climb on them. They are climbing on the bodies of those who have fallen or been driven into the mist of poison. Opposite me, they seem to be crawling up the wall. They have trampled the dead and dying and are climbing on each other. The mist is rising on them all, covering all. Suddenly I see before my own eye a bulging wide-open eye.

Tableau Number Six:

"They named it 'Canada' because of its riches," Frank says, "because it's always cold here, because it's vast and a storehouse."

We stand before a man-high pile and tangle of eyeglasses, wire frames, shattered glass. The clothes have been separated into men's and women's, jackets and pants. The piles of clothes are mountainous. I must bend my head back to see the tops.

"Would you like to try on a jacket, Malaparte? You can have your pick—tweed, flannel, the very best. Do you know what everybody does when they stand here and put on a jacket? They feel about in the pockets."

Malaparte hears glass shattering.

He is kneeling before the stove, glass lies in a thousand pieces on the wood plank floor. He turns his bulletlike head to the window, glimpsing on the floor the windup phonograph, Prince panting in a dark corner. Someone has shot the window to pieces. He hears cries, commands: "Curfew! Dim your light!"

He is lightheaded as he stands. "Come in and be welcome," he says to the two drunken Romanian soldiers standing outside the window, their rifles pointed unsteadily at him.

They tramp in, flashing their lights into the dim corners. "Pooh!" one says, holding his nose, the light on Prince.

They are high cheekboned coarse-faced young countrymen. They tramp about more noisily that he, his uniform unclean, the week's stubble on his face, is yet intimidating. "Papers!" one demands.

"Will this do?" Malaparte asks. He is amused, suspecting they cannot read. "Do you recognize Colonel Lupu's signature?" But suddenly he is uneasy. He is looking through his bag. Not the cards, not the camera. The camera is useless! "Drink?" he asks.

He has no glasses. He passes the bottle of brandy.

"It's a night of witches," one of the soldiers says, wiping his mouth with the back of his hand. His belted horse-blanket trench coat makes him seem twice as large as he is. "You'll keep your light dim when we leave, *domnule* captain. You'll stay indoors."

"Witches?" Malaparte asks, smiling.

"In the night the witches circle Jassy to call up the spirits to protect us. But if the witches find a man in their way, they cut him down!" The soldier makes the sweeping gesture of a scythe before the skirt of his coat.

Malaparte laughs. "Has the curfew been ordered because you're afraid of witches?"

Both soldiers smile that they know more than they will tell.

But Malaparte is again looking at the stove. "Is the Romanian army afraid of witches?"

They look at him cunningly. One says, "Strange things are happening in Jassy, *domnule* captain. Only yesterday, a man living alone was found murdered in his bed. There are partisans, spies."

"Do you want us to put your dog out of his misery?" the other soldier asks. "He's no good to anyone now."

The stove door is big before Malaparte's eyes, he sees through the vent the bed of ashes breathing, glowing. He glimpses sideways as if behind a veil the panting brown and white spotted hunting dog. "Never mind," he says, bending to the stove, dismissing them.

We are three in the mist, greatcoated, booted, visor-capped.

Did you ever, Frank cunningly asks the mournful spirit of the camp commandant, masturbate?

Never, the mournful spirit, always dutiful, always profound, replies.

And when you were in solitary confinement, did you put hands on yourself?

Never, the mournful spirit repeats.

And you, Malaparte?

No Italian, I answer, masturbates.

We have come far into the nighttime mist. Striped pajama-uniformed prisoners cross our path and, seeing us, scurry off. I have smelled pervasive odors in this camp-like-a-city before, but this is different. I have smelled the sweet smell we all know—and have secretly searched—of burned hair. There are times in the day that the smell of burned hair hangs everywhere over the camp, and in the commandant's flower garden one looks for the magical bush of such an aroma. But this odor is a color too. The mist is brown.

We must climb the ladder of a mirador. We are three men in greatcoats and visored hats standing behind the sweeping searchlight far above the upsteaming source of the mist, long split in the earth, deep moiling trench.

This is what they are! Frank says. They are caca! Look, he says, spreading his arms, regal gesture.

Pajama-uniformed grimacing Jews come slow-moving running in the night, their hands holding up their beltless pants, their wooden shoes clacking. Hurry, hurry, let me through. But Jews armed with sticks want payment to allow them to approach the trench. Beggar Jews would sell caca rags. And, since this is the very meeting place of all the camp, a hundred ambulatory commerces flourish here—clothes, food, money found in pockets in Canada. The running Jews straddle the trench and let go. At any time, there are a hundred straddling the trench or squatting from one side over the rising brown moil.

Do you see them? Do you blame me if we treat them like caca? Caca, I'd call to them, come here! Caca, I'd name them all. What's your name? Caca's your name!

My eye catches something strange moving among the merchants hawking their wares about the caca trench, something tender, dancing-like, like a sweeping flighted bird. It is a small man wearing rags sewn together and spangled with stars, moons, symbols of the Crab, the Bull, the Lion. He tries to stop colicky wood-shod Jews and mimes he is mute and points first to the sky and then to himself that he will read their horoscopes in the celestial tableaux caught in his robe. He will explicate, they will see. We are smiling, no one stops to buy from the imploring birdlike soothsayer knowledge of his future.

But now he is in the center of the spotlight, and he is alone there facing the very source of light behind which we three, greatcoated, leather-visored, stand even as one. And he is shielding his eyes with one hand but the other is raised that we give him our attention, that he is addressing us: Look, watch! He squats now within his sign-spangled rag-sheet robe, and now he reaches from forward like a woman underneath her skirt, and now with his finger he points toward his anus. And now he strains his caca, and he is pushing, and it is coming forth, and cupping his hands underneath him he catches his caca and it is a globe, and he stands and brings forth the caca globe like a birth, raising it toward us. Fortune! Oh, I shall read your fortunes! I shall tell you such things!

3

In the morning Malaparte awakes hungry. He wants to think that his appetite, that his desire now to be clean, is health itself.

Outside, at the rusty pump at the well, he strips to the chest and washes. He sees the tall two-door Ford. There are worn running boards beneath the doors. He shaves at the pump. Prince is now at his side, he washes the dog's long wounds. In the night, he washed them with brandy. They are not deep, they are healing. Inside the cabin, he dresses, he sweeps the room clean. Where Prince lay there are flies yet. He soaks bread in water for Prince. Prince approaches the mush and laps at it. He prepares his meal. He sets a place for himself on the floor, his pocketknife, a bottle of red wine; he sits down cross-legged on the floor, he opens and makes a spread of the newspaper-wrapped herring, the hard salami, the black bread, a hard Grana-like cheese—the very sight of which is sharp to the taste. Prince looks up reproachfully from his mush. Malaparte smiles and cuts him a slice of the salami. Prince swallows it in a gulp and waits for more.

Malaparte drinks from the bottle. And why not a little music? He winds up the phonograph. "Until tomorrow," the husky-voiced tenor sings. Malaparte sings along, "Until tomorrow, Marynona."

His teeth are going bad, his gums ache in hard chewing. He punishes his gums. The salami is good. He looks at the thick slice in his hand, the small whole black peppers, the pieces of garlic green in the dark red and pearly white substance of the salami.

Prince is growling low.

"What is it, Prince?"

Three derby-hatted dark-coated men are approaching the door. They are tax collectors, diplomats. No, they are a delegation, a committee, and the tall pale one in the middle is Boris Wienachstman. Sit down, Boris, Malaparte wants to say, I miss our games, queen's pawn four.

"Come in, gentlemen," he says without rising, taking a bite of the golden-skinned herring, a bit of black bread. "May I offer you a drink?" He raises the bottle to his lips, drinks, and then holds it out to them.

One is small and slender. "I've already eaten," he says.

Wienachtsman drinks.

"Make yourselves at home," Malaparte says ignoring the dying scratches of the phonograph. "Though I must say you look like undertakers with your hats on."

Wienachtsman removes his hat. The small and slender man removes his derby as if only in order to brush his hair back with his hand. The other removes his derby revealing a skullcap, the earlocks of an orthodox Jew falling like a woman's curls about his full sweat-glistening face. Malaparte thinks of the Jewish things the squat orthodox wears beneath his outer clothes, the stringed garments that one kisses, he thinks of the black leather bindings Jews wrap up their forearms, he sees the black box they bind by leather to their foreheads. The flesh of the squat man's face, his glistening cheeks, is firm; his large eyes, behind silver-rimmed eyeglasses, look piercingly at him.

"*Domnule* Malaparte—," Wienachtsman begins.

But the small slender man wants to go right to the heart of the matter. He is an upright man, sure of himself, proud. "We've come to ask you whether you'll act to remove the grave danger facing the Jewish community of Jassy, one thousand men, women, and children."

Malaparte picks at one of those slender herring bones caught between his teeth. "What danger?"

"Tonight or tomorrow," Wienachtsman says uneasily, "there will be a pogrom."

They are waiting to see if he is a friend of the Jews. He thinks that every Jew expects his Gentile to be an anti-Semite or Zola.

"We've given the world the patriarchs, the law."

You've given the world the Marx brothers. "You've given the world—Christianity."

"At Christmas," the small slender man says, "my clerks

thank God for my generosity. Today, they whisper to me grudgingly, 'Go and hide, you Jews are in for it now.' "

The squat man says, "The people are superstitious! They say that everything bad that happens to them comes from us!"

"The people are afraid of you," Malaparte says.

Wienachtsman says, "They know we're afraid of them. They want to hurt us because they know we're afraid of them. Yes, we're afraid! We're weak and we tremble for those we love."

"Will you speak up for us?" the squat man demands. He is a woman to his God, but a threatening finger of God to his people's enemies.

Malaparte puts his hand on Prince's taut muscled neck to still the dog. Did you know, Prince, that Zola too loved the *bas-fonds* and *bas de soie*. "I'm an Italian, not a Jew. Were I to speak up, I'd have spoken up long ago to defend the Italians. I'd have had myself locked away for speaking up for Italians."

Wienachtsman says, "*Domnule* Malaparte, I know you were in an Italian prison."

"I'd not *domnule* me."

"Italy is winning the war!" the small slender man exclaims.

"Do you think so?"

"All we're asking you to do," the squat orthodox says, "is speak to Governor-General Frank. He's a German, he's a civilized man, not like our Iron Guard trash."

"Governor-General Frank," Malaparte says, "is a very civilized man. But Governor-General Frank is busy protecting Jews in Poland."

The squat man and the small man smile at him that he knows better.

"We're prepared," the small slender man says, "to pay you for your services."

"Are you?" Malaparte asks.

Wienachtsman is looking down at his hands.

"One hundred dollars," the small slender man says.

"That's ten cents a Jew."

"Why do you make it harder?" Wienachtsman asks softly.

"Do I?"

"A hundred and fifty dollars," the small slender man says, a last offer.

Malaparte is smiling.

"There's nothing to be gained here," the small slender man says.

Before going out, Malaparte brushes down his uniform. It hangs like pajamas, but he is a big man and wears a leather-visored cap, leather boots, and is belted tight at the waist.

"Be good, Prince."

It is the bright light of early afternoon, but strangely sunless, a glow caught in a faint mist, something warm yet in the air, something chilly, the feel of cold sweat.

In the cobblestoned narrow twisting streets some stalls and stores are open, others, as early the afternoon of the eve of a holiday, are already shuttered. Even the sullen beastlike porters bent ninety degrees to the earth, brow-harnessed to the burdens platformed on their backs, have a secret light in their eyes. An artisan, hammering copper, waves Malaparte over to his stall. "A drink, *domnule* captain?"

Malaparte tips his head back and drinks from the small-lipped bottle.

95

"To Italy!" the artisan says, drinking in his turn. There is a commotion down the cobblestoned street. The artisan slips his narrow-headed hammer into his belt, his bottle into a pocket.

It is a parade, boys and men preceding it, a crowd already gathering here to watch its passing: men and kerchiefed, apronned women, baskets on their arms, children jumping in place to see better. Malaparte sees the derby-hatted head of tall Wienachtsman. They are marching the three Jewish diplomats through the streets. There is the sound of laughter, the high pitch of merriment. Every now and then a smart aleck lifts the orthodox's derby from his head so that the people can see his skullcap pinned to his hair; his curls hang down now even when his derby is fit back on his head. Sometimes the orthodox slaps at the hand reaching for his hat, and that gives the smart aleck occasion for being a moaning and whining child, and the people laugh even more. The small upright Jew looks straight ahead even as Wienachtsman. Let him alone, Malaparte wants to say of Wienachtsman. Only look my way, he wants to say, and I'll pick you out of there. Only look me in the eye. But he understands now that Wienachtsman will not look at any face that he not recognize anyone. Oh, finer than eye! And something in Malaparte wants to stand on watching this thing too. The man at Malaparte's side, the narrow-headed hammer in his belt, calls out, "No one to shine your shoes now!" And only now does Malaparte see that they are being made to walk barefoot. Some in the crowd laugh at the joke, but others are nodding gravely as if they have indeed been bending to and shining the shoes of Jews too long.

Malaparte knows that this is what he has felt in the air before. He knows it is always in the air. It leans and

96

crowds over the narrow tortuous streets that lead nowhere and it needs only a spark to set it off. It is an anger locked up in dark suffocating rooms. The people poach worm-infested wood for smoking stoves. And the people need this release from the darkness and pain, from all the burdens they must carry. This thing is in the blood, it comes from deeper than we know. Yes, Malaparte thinks, it is healthy, it is hygienic, it is the very physics of the soul!

About the Jockey Club is a loose cordon of long black leather coated and booted machine pistol–armed SS motorcyclists. Many are mounted still on their strong thick machines. Malaparte can almost feel still echoing reverberations between his own thighs. The goggles of some of the motorcyclists are raised onto their helmets, and of others hang about their necks. They wear the red armband marked with two lightning S's. They are heavy as in armor; their faces are like stone, still they glisten in the sunless light with perspiration.

Romanian officials and officers wait on the stairway in small groups of similar rank. Many are cavalry-booted. The colors of their uniforms are black, gray, and green, they are decorated with medals, ribbons, braid, gold trimming, epaulets. Tall-mitred popes stand together high on the stairs, but to a side. Their loose cloaks, covering long vestments, are embroidered with gold and silver; their beards hang to their chests; gold ruby-studded crosses large as a hand that can be raised to the lips and kissed and then raised above crowds hang low on their bodies. Uniformed schoolboys wait with their teacher just outside the cordon. One of the boys holds a giant bouquet of red and white carnations. Above the club flies a red and black swastikaed flag.

"What is it, Malaparte?" Lupu says, looking up from

papers. He is wering a fresh uniform; his hair, cut short, bristles like metal.

Malaparte does not like to be looked at as Lupu now looks at him. The young colonel will read in him the night and his breathlessness. Malaparte throws his chest out like a soldier, claps his heels to like a soldier on report, his cap is clasped hard under his arm against his side. He aims his words at a point on the wall above the colonel's head. "The same thing will happen again!" he says, but even as he speaks, he knows the reference is unclear, and his mind clouds, he feeling something forgotten rising in him. The florid-faced man is here, or is close. 'Governor-General Frank is coming to Jassy on a friendship visit,' Lupu told him. 'There'll be a dinner in his honor, a hunt. He particularly asked that you be present.' Malaparte says, "Do you want their blood on your hands?"

Now Lupu understands. He answers, "What would you have me do?"

"You can order the police to close the ghetto."

"If I do that, the people will burn the ghetto down."

"You can order the police to fire at offenders."

"Then they'll be firing on the Iron Guard, they'll be firing on our popes and monks, they'll be firing on Romanians. Do you expect us to fire on our own in order to save Jews? Why, Malaparte, this sudden feeling for Jews? I'm busy, Malaparte, is there nothing else I can do for you?"

My papers, he answers now, returning through the narrow twisting streets the way he came. Gasoline for my car. The air is heavier yet, it presses dankly against the skin, and Malaparte wonders how he will breathe if there is no air. There are few people in the streets, every shop and stall is now closed and boarded up. He wants to get out now, Mon Repos, the blue sea below. He thinks, And if ever anyone asks for me, I'll be my own concierge and step out of the ruins and say, Signor Malaparte is gone, we've had no word from him for many months. I'll wait for myself on Capri, I'll play chess with myself waiting for my own coming home. I'm not half so bad a loser when I play against myself.

He hears behind him a sound of running and shouting. A man turns a corner and now is flying down the narrow cobblestoned street toward Malaparte. Behind him come dark-uniformed men who seem in the first turning-corner instant to be huge wing-spread crowding blackbirds. The runner—as if he would be polite even in escape—slows and twists himself to avoid touching even the space about Malaparte. His eyes are wide open, his face is scratched, his mouth is gasping fishlike for air. Malaparte would know no one, Malaparte is gone, is elsewhere, still there is something familiar about this running gasping man. Already, the blackbird-like men—they are cross-belted, hatless—are cramming into each other and twirling about Malaparte like hookey-playing schoolboys discovered by their teacher, he standing in the center of the street like a statue, big, sky blue uniformed, booted, his cap leather-visored. He glimpses an acned face—hair combed back, slicked to the head as he himself once wore his hair—smiling briefly at him. He sees the boy hunched over the black and white piano keys. What music, he muses, was it? All an evening and night a music was with him, birdlike presence ever beyond reach. He wants to whistle the music, but nothing comes to mind; he bends his ear into the open well of the piano—nothing! Can't you play louder than that! It was mysterious, beautiful. The words are empty, stale. "Until Tomorrow" comes to mind, Marynona's fuzz-mustached face. If they, he considers, waving images like gnats from before his face, are off my path, I'll put them out of my mind. I'll dress for tonight, my darkest uniform, a touch of silver, high polished boots. 'Adieu,' great florid-faced Governor-General Frank will say to me tonight. 'Adieu, we shall not meet again. Remember me!' I am standing at a lectern writing, but I can see no words, and now Governor-General Frank is, like a soul in pain, reaching across a mist toward me. I am never out of my dream, there is not a minute in the day that I am not imprisoned in my dream. Before me is a crowd forming about the wing-waving blackbirds, men appearing out of doorways, men and women leaning out of windows above. Marco is in the center of the group. 'Why do you keep coming back?' he asked me in the dim glowing ghetto store, but it is he who keeps coming back! And here too is Patrice again.

Malaparte clears a way through the crowd, his shoulder-gripping touch that of authority and dignity. He hears someone whisper, "It's the Italian captain."

"Why are you tormenting this boy?" he demands, the language and tone that degree above the occasion that permits a reply.

"We're only having some fun," Patrice, black-uniformed, cross-belted, says.

"This boy is my friend," Malaparte proclaims, the meaning a complicity between him and all the crowd: He is my Jew.

"I went to school with him," Patrice says, like claiming him for himself. Malaparte looks into Patrice's face, Dimitriu-blooded and high-cheekboned proud, the deep lidding of eyes that will one day read *Noli me tangere*. Come, son, we'll mount our motorcycles and step them strongly started and roar across the world together. There's no good paternity. I'd have it that we be brothers. Listen, I'll have starlets clean that acne from your face. Nor do I want you to mourn me, let no man mourn me. "I've known him all my life," Patrice says. "He's different. He's always been different. Haven't you always been different, Marco?"

Malaparte looks at Marco who does not nod his head, and yet it is as if.

"All we want, and there's no harm involved, is to see what he looks like underneath." Patrice's voice is a plaint, a teasing song.

There are fifty people in a crowd about them in the narrow street, and more people arriving. And this is a solution. And he himself has wondered what Jews hide in their clothing. Nor will anyone lose face. Italy will be saved another loss of face, and the Iron Guard, and he and his boy, and the Jew will not be beaten.

"Show them," Malaparte agrees, shrugging. "I'm here."

Malaparte would avert his eyes, he would look at a building face, a storefront. Haglike women's faces are hanging out of windows above, strong-necked men look like butchers. He will act, profile to it all, that they are being childish. But it will not do, the Jewish boy too is perhaps looking elsewhere, the thing in his hand. Malaparte must look as he has always looked. The boy's penis is small, soft, flaccid on his palm outside the buttons of his fly.

"They cut them up and sew them back together," someone observes.

Everyone is looking down at the thing, craning toward it, studying, on the brink of something deeper.

But a kerchiefed aproned woman calls from the crowd, "It's not grown, throw it back into the pond!"

"It's a woman's thing!" another woman says as if in response. And men and women are laughing.

"This will do!" Malaparte says, shielding the boy that he button up.

But Patrice is looking at Malaparte that this will do only for now.

Malaparte holds the boy's arm as he walks off with him. He leans down to him to, for the sake of the still laughing crowd behind, give him a stern talking to. He says, "Why are you out on the streets today?" But he is already smiling at himself because the next question is, Why aren't you hiding? and after that, What's wrong with you Jews, why are you always in trouble? Let him go, he tells himself. You've other brands in the fire. And indeed, all the boy finds to say is, "Why did you interfere?"

Malaparte laughs. "Come," he says, "you're not safe on these streets."

He will take him back to the cabin with him. He will think up something for him. But already his mind is elsewhere; he is thinking of the people in the street, their first quiet study as they looked at the thing. He thinks of the hair-slicked-back acne-faced boy's hate and scorn. It was his own, it is his own.

"But I'm not fair," the boy says as if he has been waiting for an answer. "I ask you questions but I say nothing of myself."

4

There is again the beginning of fever below the skin of Malaparte's forehead, little flames of energy, a troubling sense of caverns. He wonders if he did not bring the boy back here to the cabin to distract himself from his fever. He drinks brandy from the bottle. It is already the approach of evening. He must dress and prepare for the banquet. He breathes deeply, his chest fills out, he is a big man.

The boy sits cross-legged on the floor against a wall. He is never at ease, not even the occasional times when he stops talking for a moment or two. When he entered the cabin, he stood waiting near the center, a little distance from the stove, as if too timorous to risk a relationship even with a thing before being asked. Prince, now back again in his corner, resting like a sphinx on his belly, paws forward, stood growling at his feet. "Be good, Prince." Malaparte pumped water from the well, stood the boy at the stove where he put the basin of water, and washed the scratches from his face. He sees himself now, though he knows that was before, standing at the boy's side looking down into his face.

The boy has a small soft belly that he lets hang. When he loses track of his thought, he looks down at his hands and says as if modestly, "I wonder why I did that." Sometimes he looks at Malaparte, sometimes he speaks into space, sometimes the pupil of an eye swoons up out of sight leaving him mechanically finishing a sentence, searching something fleeting in an internal sky. Sometimes it seems to Malaparte that he expects him to address him, but then he starts up again as if Malaparte's silence is appropriate.

So, as the boy speaks, Malaparte moves about largely in the spreading shadows of the cabin, listening half. He stands once as if before his open wardrobe, his many pairs of shoes. The advantage of choosing a uniform is the unity of choice, one does not have to decide on accessories.

Though, even with a uniform, there are some choices and each can be weighty. He lights the lamp, the smell of brandy burning. He offers the boy the bottle to drink from. Of course he refuses. Your father drank with me. His collar is too tight. He has learned that he must accept every dark card he turns up, but he is a dark card. He considers that now that the suffocation has begun, it will never cease. He must close the shutter of the broken window, he must prepare food for Prince. He is standing over his bag, what is he looking for?

The issue is choice, the issue is always choice. He shall strike a blow that shall be heard throughout Europe!

The boy is, like all such interior people, fascinated by his complexity, delighted to speak of it, showing off both his knowledge and himself.

"I began with theory. It was a wonderland. Everything had meaning, and each meaning opened up the door to another meaning. I'd open a book and have to read every sentence twice; the subject was me, it took my breath away. And then, continuing to read, I began to analyze my dreams. I passed in my study and in my dreams from stage to stage. I discovered the origins of my feelings. My music, how I played, even how I sat at the piano, changed. My father wanted to pull me back, but then he began to watch me as if I were risking my life as he might have wanted to. I was a hero in my mind as I uncovered my mind. I opened doors and there were monsters and my facing them was like a hero's facing a monster. I was a hero, but my territory was too large. A man's life, his past in the present, is too deep, is too much. But I'm speaking too generally—."

Malaparte, sitting cross-legged now like the boy, his back to the same wall as the boy's, the stove that he sat facing the night before an empty point equidistant from them, the shutter on the broken window closed, the lamp smoking and flickering, the air in the cabin cold, dank, and close about them, is thinking again of choices, he is organizing the evening in his mind, and something in him is telling him even now that he will not do it, that the thing which now seems to him great he will know then to be only vain, as he has ever been vain, only boastful, as he has ever been boastful, mask and disguise on something worse. But still, even as he is thinking, he is listening, fascinated as if he were the boy and the boy were holding his penis yet in the open palm of his hand. He thinks there is no shame. He thinks, smiling, there is no shame even as there is no horror. To whom is he boasting now? The real horror, he will say, is the absence of horror. But he knows then, like almost seeing it, that the giant worm in him is only waiting to thrust its swallowing jaws out of his mouth. He is smiling thinking that the stonelike silence and immobility of Prince, sphinx in the corner, is the deep one of jealousy. He is smiling that in the Jockey Club they are putting the finishing touches to the banquet tables, flowers! that in the streets the diplomats are walking naked, and that here in the cabin they are talking of Jack-the-giant-killer. He is looking straight ahead, restraining himself from tearing at his collar, listening to the boy at his side, thinking that the Jews are naked wearing leather bindings, frilled corded things that hang against their bodies. They are walking, their heads bowed, furtive, their hands cupped before their sex.

"Like every boy child, I sometimes hated my father—the principle, if I understand it correctly, is that the son is always jealous of the mother's love, of any attention she gives anyone else. But at the same time, I knew—Father's Law!—it was wrong to hate my father, and perhaps in order to be able to love him, and perhaps for what remained of my hate for him—that I be despised by him—and surely to ever possess my mother, I identified with my mother. If I say that my playing piano, or the way I play piano, is a result of this, I'll be simplifying, but still, I'll not be far from the truth. . . . You find me, what I say, distasteful?"

I don't know, Malaparte does not say, if it's you, or Prince, or me, who smells so. He says, "You should play a sport, something to get you out-of-doors."

The boy is nodding. "All my life, first unconsciously, and then consciously, I've thought I was a woman. I thought my breasts were a woman's breasts, my—." He stops himself, a pupil of an eye swoons up. He must compose himself before resuming. "I thought my body was a woman's body. My music is only that. I put all my love on music, music couldn't hurt me, and what I now discover is that my music is twisted, is disease. My love is nothing, never outside of me. My very hands are twisted. . . . I stood in a crowd watching them laugh at and torment my father. I stood there and there was a crying shouting need in me to pull together, to do something, to make out of all the different parts of me one *man,* not a hero, just a man, able to reach out, to speak up, to initiate. But I know that to be a man, I must first throw off something of me, some identity like a skin, some sweetness in me that I don't want to get rid of. I stood by as they tormented my father and I said nothing. I began to edge off, and one stopped me, but I said, 'I'm a Christian, let me go.' And I think I wanted my father to see and hear, like punishing him, like punishing me, Mal-a-parte! My language is no good. It's too deep for living in this world. I've had to hide my knowledge, there are words I'm afraid to use even to myself, that I might fall in love with them! I've had to hide my knowledge, I've not permitted myself to speak of it to others, because it offends, because it reduces everything to dust. It's a language too precise for this world. But hiding the language in me, I transformed, I became it. It should, some people say—my language, my knowledge—give equilibrium to a person, but it's killed every illusion and offers nothing in place, only the truth, only itself. I'm in a bad way. The normal man, don't you see, projects the woman in him into the form of his mother, his sister, his wife. But I've made the woman me. I love only me, my love is all twisted in on me and it's like hate. That's why I admire you. You're a man, you did what I couldn't do, you stepped in."

Oh, you fool! Take in your hands! Take the world in your hands and do, and be. Taste the world with your mouth, love it with your body. And still he feels an affection for the boy. "I stepped in," he explains, "because it didn't matter. Had it really mattered, I'd have stood by."

The boy looks at him questioningly. But now he says, "I don't think so."

"Had my skin been at issue, I'd have stood by." He is telling the truth, but it is a lie as all words must be lies. I want to stand by. Every sight I see makes me know that I am alive, and every sight that I see is a story, and the stronger the sight, the better the story, the more I triumph.

"I don't think you would have stood by."

The boy looks, cross-legged, like a sage. Malaparte studies the pale whiteness of his skin. He thinks there is a white radiance to his skin like something one unwraps from the dead. He is again in his mind standing by the stove looking down at the boy's scratched face. And he is suddenly faint thinking, I interfered because I didn't want my boy to do worse to you than I'd have him do to me.

"I'd like to help you," the boy says, such a modesty in his tone, such discretion, that Malaparte does not laugh outloud. He leans forward and to a side to look into the flickering-light lit face of this new hypnotist: the pupil of one eye has again swooned up out of sight, leaving only the sickly white, and the pupil of the other eye is half-lidded, unfocused.

"Your father came to me for help. I refused him. I saw your father walking barefoot in the street, I did nothing."

"Would it be easier for you to talk if I were really a woman?"

The boy is rocking forward and back; his eyes are now closed, he is reaching so hard. Malaparte is touched by this reaching and would pity the boy, but then he wonders, Would I confess more easily to a woman than a man? What is he really saying? And again he feels a flame of anger for this probing in him, nothing is revealed. He drinks. He wipes his mouth with the back of his hand, already he is thirsty.

"Is it because of who I am, of what you've seen of me, of what I've told you?" The boy is nodding an answer to his own questions. "Of course! How can you think I can help you? There's a distance between us that's uncrossable. You won't accept from me, you hardly see me. How can I be more than a shadow to you? How can someone like me help anyone else, much less a man like you, who can *do* things, who's meant to do things. Of course, it must be me who crosses to you, it must be me who talks to you!"

The distance would be less, Malaparte is thinking, if you'd only open your eyes, if you could see me. "Have a drink," Malaparte again offers, stretching the bottle to him encouragingly. But the boy only smiles wanly, recognizing the pity.

"There's an uncrossable distance between us, and you're already going on your way and why should you look back at me, and the only way is for me to cross to you now. If I could only help you, everything would again have a sense. What's happened to me is that once we begin to look in on ourselves, we get locked into ourselves. What's the way out, where's the key? I'm always standing at the edge, watching others, watching myself standing at the edge, blaming, criticizing. I've done that so much with my father that in my mind there's nothing left of him, only my fantasies of him! If I ever do anything, it's only to prove to myself that I'm alive, and is always to fail, to prove to me that I'm nothing, that I'm all alone in the world. Whatever love I have is twisted. No, I'm unable to love. I think I'm the very absence of love."

Malaparte says, "The word you'd not say before is *anus*." He is smiling warmly, affectionately, that he has been uncovering that all this time, that he knows this too of the boy.

The boy, looking blindly ahead, frowns at the word.

Malaparte is tempted to touch the boy. We are both the absence of love, we are both shadows. Still, the other temptation is to tell the story. Of the magical ring. The musical bird of all the songs, the caca bird. He shall sing the caca bird at the banquet table this evening. Prophet bird, he thinks, moody.

"Do you know how I'd give concerts? Behind a folding screen. I'm on a stage hidden by a folding screen from my audience. Oh, I don't want them to see me. I play with my back to them. But, oh, I do so want them to hear my music!"

The boy is like a dying glow in the cabin, and Malaparte is already thinking elsewhere. He is standing facing a mirror cutting with nail scissors the hairs in his nostril.

"There must be a way out! If only I could look at the real you, if only I could really address you! If only one man could do for another what each man must do! If only I were man enough to assume all of me! Now! *Anus* is the word, but in itself it's nothing, it's only memory. It resurges from our memory and it is of us, but it is not us, or, we must make it so that it is not us! *Domnule* Malaparte, if only you could believe me, you are not a bad man."

Malaparte is laughing.

"Be good, Prince," Malaparte says, turning to the dog, ready to go.

But Prince will not acknowledge his good-bye.

Malaparte smiles thinking Prince is still jealous. He bends to caress his neck. It is hard as stone and Malaparte knows that the dog knows that he is abandoning him.

"I can drive you beyond the gypsy camp," Malaparte says to the boy.

The boy is standing in the doorway. He has been watching Malaparte standing by Prince. Now the pupil of one eye swoons up leaving the eye blind. He has reached as hard as he could. He says, his whole body now a drawing back, a backing out the door, "We did almost begin to make progress, didn't we?"

Were I a German, Malaparte thinks, looking at the lidded-eyed sphinxlike spotted dog in the dim flickering light of the cabin, the boy gone, I'd poison you now.

He drives his Ford heavy, slow, lumbering, in the labyrinth-like twisting dark streets of Jassy. Ahead, a man comes running around a corner, but, seeing the headlights of the car, stops and turns back. Already, turning the corner, comes a troop of men, some carrying torches trailing sparks, a cry echoing in the air, Get the Jew!

He parks across the square from the big-windowed Jockey Club. Chandeliers glow within. Three Mercedes limousines are parked at the steps; the cordon of helmeted black leather coated SS stands like stone. The schoolchildren are gone but inside now there will still be about the barrel-chested shining-booted Deutsches Konig vom Poland the fragrance of red and white flowers, it will stick to him, to his glowing cheeks, like eau de cologne. He will smile seeing Malaparte, he will excuse himself to the nobles and notables he stands with and come, shining boots clicking, across the parquet floor. For he is a king who will be known for his culture, who will be a protector of the arts, and he has been his very guide and mentor. And Malaparte will bow to him and play still by the rules, I shall say nothing until the truth rises from within me.

Lupu's Romanian soldiers are hurriedly saluting Malaparte in. He is late. The red-jacketed dwarflike doorman, standing behind the shoulder of a fair-haired German lieutenant busy with papers at an entry table, whispers his name into the lieutenant's ear. The lieutenant looks up blushing.

"Where's your violin, lieutenant?" Malaparte asks, remembering him, veiled picture in his mind, the lieutenant languishing, a violin trailing from his hand on the floor.

The lieutenant, handing him a place number, looks into his eyes like asking him to try to understand something so large and deep, so new even to him, that he himself knows it cannot be understood. But Malaparte is feverish and this boy too is from another time, another place. He too, he remembers now, played piano. He smiles at him to reassure him that he is beautiful, fair, soft. A Romanian soldier salutes him and says, "Your arm, *domnule* captain." Malaparte chooses not to hear.

He stands at the threshold of the large banquet room. He is shining booted, his visored cap is clasped to his side under his arm, one eye squints for the other that in his mind is monocled. Here all is movement and color, rosy animated faces, bouquets of red and white carnations, rich red Bulgarian roses in tall vases, olives with hearts of red, almost liquid, pepper. The white cloth sets every color off, glassware and silver gleam. A hundred wine goblets are filled with a champagne-like red drink. And there is the king, his monk's crown of short blond hair, his pinpoint blue eyes. He has brought members of his court, aides-de-camp, SS, and, of course, the cream of Jassy nobility and notability is here. The countess is seated a little distance down from Frank, but one can feel her presence, her veiling glow, about all the head of the table. Malaparte feels a melancholy in the pit of him that she is here, and yet he knew she would be. But now a half-silence is falling over the room, talk continuing, the tone lower, the women—in peach and pink organdy, bare shoulders gleaming—, the men—in black uniforms decorated with silver, badges of red, in dinner clothes—, glancing at Malaparte. The Romanian soldier comes from behind. "Your arm, *domnule* captain," he insists.

"My arm?" Malaparte asks, offended.

"I've orders," the soldier says, tense and trembling that everyone can see he has not carried them out.

Colonel Lupu stands from the table and approaches.

Everyone is attentive. He has been Malaparte.

"Are you afraid even of Italians?" he asks Lupu who is a head shorter than he.

Lupu looks at him as if he is tired of humoring him. Lupu looks at him from beneath the appearance of humoring him, searching. Frank looks on severely from the head of the table. Malaparte bows to the countess and then raises his arms high in the air like a prisoner that the soldier disarm him.

The soldier opens the flap of Malaparte's pistol holster and extracts a crumpled packet of Lucky Strike.

"Ah! That takes the cake!" Malaparte exclaims. "Those cigarettes were put there. Italians are not black marketeers!"

Women are smiling behind their fans. They know a joke when they hear one. He is being naughty, Malaparte, *enfant terrible.* The countess is smiling faintly. He wonders, Have you too forgiven me? So soon? Still, what are you doing here among these shopkeepers' wives! He is looking about at the faces here. He looks at an SS, small thin eyeglassed man, birdlike head made to peck, bookkeeper, into pages. He thinks of professions as animals. The squat Iron Guard colonel began life as a butcher, cleaving through meat. Where are the eagle faces of the nobility? Clip its wings and a bird is a rat.

"Give him back his arm!" Frank commands, standing before him, florid cheeks glowing, the fragrance of flowers.

Now they are laughing at Malaparte. The soldier is smiling, he stuffs the packet of cigarettes back into the holster.

Frank is looking Malaparte up and down. "Colonel Lupu," he asks, "why is this man in pajamas?"

Malaparte says, "These are not pajamas! This is the uniform of the Italian army!"

"Then you're an army of sleepwalkers and black marketeers! You!" he calls to the dwarf looking on from behind. "Put a bed down for the sleepwalker." The dwarf is grinning from ear to ear. Malaparte is being punished. The grown-ups are at table. He has been put to bed without dinner. He will write a book! Their derbies and monocles, their fast carriages seen between the narrow white birch trees like a film at off-speed. The fuzz-mustached maid will come to bring him a taste of their dinner. Hearts of pigeon like tiny fruit in a cream sauce. What profession with an apple caught between its teeth will be brought out for the main course? *Deutsches Konig!* She will, slender, come to him while he sleeps, silver hair glowing, the rustle of her crepe-aged white gown, the tips of her small silver shoes, and bend to him and touch his brow with her lips. No. They are doctors and dentists gathered at the table, it is his operation they are preparing. He looks up and he sees the head of the boar.

"*Vas ist das?*" he demands, cross-legged on his mattress on the floor, a goblet of the red drink in his hand.

"Malaparte talks German in his sleep!" Frank says, and the whole table roars with laughter. "That is *Turkisch Blut!* It's what hunting men drink in Germany before the hunt."

"Are you sure it's Turkish blood?"

"Malaparte thinks French champagne and burgundy too thin for Turkish blood!"

"In any event, it's not German blood."

"Of course it's not German blood. We are the hunters! Tomorrow we shall corner and kill the boar!"

"*Prosit!*" Malaparte calls, studying then the stuffed head of the beast, reminder only of the huge breathing stinking razor-backed beast he saw in the forest. The fiery eyes, the spiny hairs that can pierce, the tusks that with the wet leathery snout swing up out of the earth, the mass of it like a hurtling stinking meteor released up out of the earth, the groan rising like a cry. He thinks for an instant that the steamy presence of the beast is here, it has wan-

dered out of the forest and in a dewy dawnlike silence
entered the Jockey Club.

"You are dreaming!" Governor-General Frank, at the
head of the table, calls out to Malaparte near the bottom
of the table.

Malaparte is studying the *Turkish Blut*. He says, "I
thought for a minute this was Jewish blood."

"It's too fine for Jewish blood!" Frank says. "Look at
it, it bubbles. Does Jewish blood bubble?"

Malaparte thinks that the eyeglassed bookkeeper is
smiling numbers, that the *S*'s on his armband are infinite
sevens.

"Jewish blood is like pure spring water," Malaparte
says. "The Jews, in fact, are very fine. Like women, they
think that because we martyrize them, they're better than
us."

"Look about you, Malaparte! Do these women re-
mind you of Jews? Is there one woman here who reminds
you of a Jew? Would they deny their children?"

Malaparte asks, looking up and down the long table at
every woman's face, "Is there not one of you who sits up
through the night playing solitaire?"

He is looking at the countess.

"Will you not speak up for the Jews?"

There is a silence. The countess is a wounded eagle.

The SS asks, "What, Captain Malaparte, do you want
to be said for the Jews?"

"That they shouldn't die like women, their hands before their sex."

"It takes a man to die like a man!" Frank says.

"I've seen Reichsfuehrer Himmler die like a woman."

"Reichsfuehrer Himmler die like a woman?" the SS
repeats in a whisper tight with menace.

"I saw him in a sauna in Finland. When all the men began to birch each other, I saw Himmler cover his breasts and his sex with his hands."

Frank would smile at the story, but he frowns severely. He likes Malaparte, he competes with him, but he is the king and he must always win. His favor protects Malaparte, the boy is ungrateful. "Malaparte is obsessed," he explains to the SS. "He loves women so much, he is falling in love with the Jew!"

Malaparte bows his head, It is true.

Frank continues: "Twenty years ago, we came home from the last war, and our medals were worthless and we had no future. Money was worthless, only speculators lived well. Malaparte blamed the bourgeoisie, his ideal was even ours, that the world be a larger place, spacious, noble, fearless, pure. But he did not see that the sickness wasn't the bourgeoisie, but the Jew. That it was Jewish values that corrupt, Jewish cunning, the very Jewish blood. And now, when all of Europe is ours, England on the verge of capitulation, our forces in Russia on the point of surrounding and destroying a Russian army of a million men, when the New Order is finally here, giving meaning to our every gesture, he will speak still of Jews. They shall fade, Malaparte, even from our memory!"

"Reichsfuehrer Himmler was never in a sauna," the SS insists.

"No doubt," Malaparte agrees.

"Silence!" Frank commands, glaring. "We are the New Order of Knighthood and there is no room for this kind of talk. We are loyal or we are nothing!" He has turned to Colonel Lupu. "Isn't that so, Colonel Lupu?"

Malaparte looks from face to face at this long table of Iron Guard patriots, and Romanian and Germany army officers, and SS, and Romanian politicians and noblemen, and almost all are belted and girdled tight. And even Frank, he knows, has aims not quite those of other German leaders. Himmler put a hundred Polish intellectuals against the wall, Frank saved fifty.

"There are some Romanians," Frank continues ominously, "who've chosen to support the Russians!"

The Iron Guard colonel is staring triumphantly at Lupu. Lupu says, "There's a band of deserters in the forest. In the night, they come out of the forest and—steal chickens!"

"The Third Reich," Frank intones, "will not stand for duplicity. When you choose us, it's a blood choice! Not for a day or a year, but for the thousand years of the Third Reich!"

"The Third Reich is immortal!" the Iron Guard colonel, standing, declares like a heil.

Women are trembling with emotion. Men stand to show their loyalty.

Malaparte's bald bullet head is bent and nodding over the table. He says, the soft tone of his voice like a last echo of the heil, "That's the difference between the communist and the German. The communist lives only in history, the German in immortality. One would be a fool to be anything but German."

"The difference," Frank corrects, "is that one is civilized and the other is a barbarian. The German's culture is unsurpassed, the German is civilized and is at home among civilized people."

The table bows to Frank's compliment.

"The Russians, however," Malaparte says, "are generous."

Frank frowns. "The Russians generous?"

"Marshal Kutuzov, fighting the Poles, said to his soldiers, 'We'll leave them only their eyes—for them to weep with!' "

"That is Russian generosity!"

"But your hetman, Pavelic, when I spoke with him, had a barrel in his office filled with oysters. I've met a hundred chiefs of state, but I'd never before met one who had a barrel of oysters in his office. We talked of this and that, and he was always smiling a little, as at a private joke. I thought that he perhaps distributed oysters to his heroes. And then I began to realize that those things were held together not by pearls but by pupils, and that those things were a thousand eyes swimming in brine, looking up at me, Pavelic laughing. 'They are,' Pavelic explained, 'the eyes of captured partisans.' "

"Pavelic," Frank says sternly, "is not a German. He's a Croat and no one has ever said that Croats are civilized. You've seen many things, Malaparte, but not even you can tell a story of Germans cutting out the eyes of enemies, not even of Jews!"

"It's true," Malaparte says, "the Germans are civilized. They don't cut out their enemies' eyes, but they collect the Jews' eyeglasses!"

Frank is laughing. "It's true, it's true!" And Malaparte is laughing too. They are all laughing, men and women— the light glittering off eyeglasses, flushed faces—, some not even knowing why, but the force of Governor-General Frank's and Malaparte's laughter carrying them all.

An army of waiters serves small headless wood pigeons and turtledoves. The birds have been roasted and basted and their skin is hard and glistens. One carves the bird into halves, they barely fill the plate. One carves slices from the breast, one pries up the small tender king's portion. It would be bad taste to take big bites, one tastes and delects the juicy thick meat and the thin. A woman squirms in her chair and decides to take the tiny drumstick in her fingers; like a squirrel, she holds the tiny drumstick to her teeth. Now others, as if at a dare, raise the tiny drumsticks to their teeth. And now a man among them begins to crack with his teeth the fragile bone that he grinds into the meat.

The chandeliers above are a thousand glass pieces reflecting the light of electric bulbs. The light turns, moves, glitters.

Frank pours for his neighbors, a bottle in each hand, the bubbly champagne and deep red burgundy.

"Do you know," Malaparte asks the countess up the table from him, "how they catch such small birds in nets? Why should a bird fly so low that it can be caught in a net?" The countess, the faint glow of her silver hair, is looking straight in front of her, her large eyes are unblinking. "Hidden in thickets between the net poles are caged decoy birds who sing night and day. Hunters learned long ago that by stinging out the eyes of a bird with a red-hot needle, the bird will sing incessantly, beautifully, urgently. The blind bird flies, time and again, into the bars of its cage, and it sings, attracting hundreds of other birds, until it dies."

"We do not hunt like that," a monocled gentleman says. "The hunt, in Romania, is civilized."

"You don't hunt with sticks and stones in Romania?"

"The hunt, with its rules and stages, is a very measure of a civilization."

"I'd think in a real civilization women would hunt and men stay home. . . . Of course, countess, these are Romanian birds, and they weren't caught like that. Do you know, countess, how they kill these small birds?" He works the forefinger of one hand like a head and neck into the noose of the forefinger and thumb of the other hand, and then suddenly rips the head off.

"Why must you hurt me?" the countess asks.

"Do you know why we kill Jews?" Malaparte asks, smiling hard, turning from her. "Every time we kill a Jew, we kill something in ourselves. Every time we watch a Jew being beaten or humiliated—

> We kill them here,
> we kill them there,
> we kill them everywhere—

The problem is, there aren't enough Jews to go around. The problem is, no matter how many we kill, the thing's still in us. Will you, Governor-General Frank, order the pogrom stopped?"

Frank says, watching, smiling, large, "I'm German, Malaparte, not Romanian. What happens in Jassy is strictly a local affair."

Malaparte takes from his jacket pocket his Beretta pistol. He points it, lying small in his hand, at Frank.

Frank has turned pale but is smiling still. No one moves.

The countess sighs his name, "Curzio."

But now Malaparte picks the pistol up by its barrel and holds it out to Lupu who only waits, immobile, alert. "If you wanted me to come unarmed, you should have told me before I came."

Frank is laughing, nodding. "Malaparte," he announces, "has always been a sporting man! Keep your pistol!" he commands Malaparte. Still, he then whispers to whoever will hear, "It's only a lady's pistol!"

The main course is venison, the small young deer

brought in on a silver platter by four sweating waiters. Except for the head and legs, the deer was skinned, and then it was spit and roasted over embers, and then the skin, singed for the presentation, glistening with fat, was hung back over the naked animal. The deer's legs are folded under it, the head rests moodily on the breast, a silver arrow has been pierced into the bullet wound in its neck. Was the animal shot in one of its wonderful bounding leaps? Did they have a battue in the forest to drive it forward? Did it turn and first stare at the hunter like a discovered wide-eyed girl?

Frank accepts the silver carving knives and forks. He draws back the deer's coverings and masterfully carves large thick slices from the animal's haunches and breast. "Light meat? Dark?" he calls convivially. He insists that everyone eat as he or she is served, and little by little an almost religious silence falls on the room as everyone eats his portion of pink tender juicy meat. Malaparte stares at his portion and then, looking up, brings his finger to his lips and says, "Sh! I hear singing."

And as everyone holds his breath and listens, there is a distant sound from outside like a wailing in a chimney.

Frank says, "You'd have us think that even a deer is a woman!" He is looking then down at his hands, medium to the deepest place of his soul, and his concentration is stilling the singing silence, and it seems that he is hearing, or that he himself is somehow on the point of becoming, another music, crescendoing final music, music of the gods.

But suddenly all regards turn upward—the chandelier lights are fading out. In every direction, the lights are gone, though now, in anterooms, there are the beams of flashlights. Men are standing from table, a young officer enters the room and approaches Lupu. People strain to hear the whispered report. Lupu's voice, issuing then quiet commands to officer guests, is reassuring. Someone laughs. Through the windows, where some of the men group now, they see a crescent moon veiled in a misty sky, and then they see, beyond rooftops, reflecting off the golden domes of churches, tall licking flames.

Servants bring candelabrum, the small flames lighting large, the flames seen through the windows like reflections only of the candles. The candelabrum are placed on the long table and on sideboards; the light, flickering at the table, glitters above off the diamond-cut chandelier pieces. Officers report to Lupu. There are quieter comings and goings about the Iron Guard colonel. Lupu addresses the guests: "There's disorder in the streets, but we are containing it." His manner and voice are so calmly in control everyone is relieved. But now, with the hundred candles here, the thick smell of falling wax, the room grows hot and a torpor comes over Malaparte.

He hears a growing glorious music and looks up. This is the music of his youth—courage, strength, will, death. Men and women, called by the music, are rising from the table—Malaparte sees on the table the moody-headed deer naked to the bone—, the women's organdy dresses become gossamer, like moth wings. The countess, holding up the train of her gown with one hand, holds a three-branched candelabra out from her body with the other. The light precedes her like her own radiance; her hair glows like burning silver. All down the long music room, men and women are standing leaning forward, angels holding their candles like burning cities to illuminate the German governor-general.

The governor-general is ploughing open the earth, splitting the sky. His fine-fingered hands, wax-red in the light, cross and recross, pound from the right, trumpet from the left, and everyone here is one breathing longing, and Malaparte sees the countess glowing and breathing fast, and she looks at him and appeals silently across a distance to him, for him, What does it matter, it's all only dream. And she is telling him, proud melancholy eagle face, Only allow yourself to believe! But the odor of melting wax is rising too thickly as if from the floor and he is pulling again at his collar, and he is gasping for air, staggering out. He glimpses in the anteroom the dwarflike doorman, his smile of complicity and knowing grotesquely boyish in the dim light. The beautiful German lieutenant, hesitant an instant, rises from the entry table he sits at and is following him outside. "*Signor* Malaparte," he begins, like pulling at a sleeve. "*Signor* Malaparte," he insists, "they are wolves, they are all wolves!" Here, midway down the steps of the Jockey Club, his lungs bursting, Malaparte breathes deeply, but the air is filled with acrid smoke that burns his lungs. The cottony sky is streaked with red, the moon is a misted keyhole. He sees at the foot of the steps, beyond the Romanian soldiers now guarding the entry, but within the cordon of helmeted, long black leather coated SS, Marynona, big, kerchiefed, aproned. She has been waiting for him here, and now she drops to her knees and looking up so steeply at him, she cries, "*Domnule* captain, you must come with me!" He has seen himself dropping to his knees to beg her forgiveness. I promise I won't be bad. Come, Marynona, to my orchard. "*Domna* Elena, she'll die if you don't make her stop!"

The lieutenant has paled and now follows swiftly after Malaparte who is striding at the side of the running Marynona.

These narrow cobblestoned labyrinth streets are dark

and airless though the sky above is a red cotton. Now and then swift bands of men and women pass shrilly ahead or behind, they carry torches, long sticks, glittering knives. Once, Malaparte feels they are being drawn in a draft, that Marynona is leading him toward the belly of the fire. The beast, he thinks, is here. The beast is charging invisible down these cobblestoned streets. The morning hunt will be here, the massing uniformed hunters mounted tall, the dog pack yelping for release, the hunt captain raising his bugle to his lips.

"Where are you taking us, Marynona?" Malaparte asks. His hand aches for her warm hairy places. Once again, Marynona. I promise I'll be good this time.

The ghetto is in flames. The scurrying forms he glimpses have come from the ghetto. The beast is turning corners, scattering people in every direction. Tall ghetto buildings are burning straight up like haystacks. "Where are you taking us, Marynona?" Why don't you speak for yourself, Marynona? Soldiers salute them. "Not this way, *domnule* captain," one says pointing and then bringing his finger to his lips like waiting for something about to happen. Down the street, Malaparte sees huddling forms and hears then a bird-shrill shouting as a torch-bearing band turns a corner and throws its long shadows like ink on the others.

Now they are beyond the labyrinth streets, in fields at the outskirts of town, and there, kneeling and mourning in a field, is Elena.

The sky behind them is full of flame and flame-tinted smoke, and she is a half-lit form profiled and rocking against the night, greatcoated still, tentlike, her legs spread wide.

In the night, smiling and tall, twinned with the other, she wore a field cap. It is gone, her long dark hair is matted and hangs madly, she has torn hair from her head, her large eyes are full lidded, bulging lidded on worlds we cannot see. Her long high cheekboned face is streaked and caked with earth and tears; her long slender fingers have scratched at her cheeks and scratched at the earth and they are bent and hard now like claws. Her lips that were a hundred wet and glistening muscles are cracked dry and dead, and the sound she makes with her every inhalation and exhalation is a deep upward and downward groaning. She is kneeling and rocking broad to the earth— the ample skirts of her greatcoat tenting even to her boots—like a woman giving birth, and she has been groaning like this all through the day, and all through the day she has been reaching into the earth and gestating it through her body.

Now Malaparte sees a long form lying limp across from Elena. It is greatcoated Pauli, her body seeming longer than a body can be, her face bloodless white, the ash blond hair spread out from her head on the ground. Her lips are cracked and whitened even as Elena's, her eyes full lidded. He sees a circle of blood that has risen through her greatcoat midway down its length. Her hands lie at her sides. There is a deep solemnity in the distance between her and her greatcoated spread-legged rooted rocking mourner, the reflected pallor, the veiled crescent moon, Marynona standing bowed behind Elena.

"Elena! Elena!" the lieutenant cries helplessly, forgiving and begging forgiveness. He drops to his knees at Elena's side. "Elena!" he implores. But there is something in her mourning that makes him and what he feels insignificant, that he leans toward her but dares not touch her. "You taught me everything I know," he murmurs.

Malaparte sees the flames over Jassy rising straight

into the sky. And he can almost see behind Elena's lidded eyes the rising of a god.

But now he bends and opens the skirt of Pauli's coat. Marynona, low like an animal to the ground, pulls at his arm, No. He knows then, *I* was the man watching. And even as he begins to smile, he remembers the dark heavy form pulling the plough through the earth, releasing the spirits that would purify Jassy. Marynona is pulling at his hand and she is staring at him now even as if she sees him then, and her face twists and knots, and her eyes are fiery, and he is pulling his hand back from her, but she will not let go, and now she springs forward and her head is bent over their hands and her teeth snap on his finger and the pain is sharp, and she has bitten off the end of his finger and the blood is pulsing from it as from a mouth. He is big, he is tottering, Holy Marynona, what have you done now! She is circling him low as if to charge again. He kicks at her. The lieutenant, kneeling still by Elena—she rocking and groaning back and forth—does not know what to do, which way even to look. Malaparte staggers off.

He is lost in the labyrinth-like cobblestoned streets of Jassy, a breathing thickness about him, flames glowing in the mist of acrid smoke. He feels the air being pulled past him into the fire, he feels the hot breath of the fire. He thinks he will, turning a corner, come upon the breathing beast. But now he hears the metal echoing clattering of a trotting horse. A Jew comes racing past him. A bare-chested horseman appears glistening over the dark form of a horse, a long chain swings from his hand. The horse-man swings his chain into the Jew's back like a game to race him forward, and the Jew flies forward but then falls onto the cobblestones, his back broken, blood bubbling out from where his head lies.

He hears horses galloping in the streets this way and that, a singing sawing music in their whinnying. He sees in a descending narrow street a group of men bent toward the ground, a man holding a torch aloft. Their arms are wings, rising and falling, beating. He sees now that their pants are open, they are ready, like dogs, to fall on all fours on their prey. He hears a chant and turns from the men—their arms stopped in air—and sees coming down the narrow cobblestoned street a procession of long-robed monks in a glow of torchlight like an arching passage. Their heads are hooded and bent, they swing, like sweeping clean, smoking censers before them. Tall bearded mitred popes are in the center of the procession. The monks' falsetto voices recite prayers and the popes answer in a deep tomblike bass. The men kneeling bow their heads and the popes, stepping blindly past them, sprinkle with jeweled crosses holy water on all. The street smells now of sweet incense.

Malaparte, lost, walking slowly that he not stagger, a nausea of faintness in him, a pulsing at his fingertip, his hand garroting the finger, turns a corner and there is Hitler himself. A little man stands hand on hip in the center of a narrow street, he has a Hitler mustache, his hair is combed down over his forehead like Hitler's, he has the high little belly of Hitler.

"Heil Hitler!" the man calls, raising and throwing back his hand as Hitler does. It is a Jew holding a black comb under his nose.

"Heil Hitler!" Malaparte calls, all of him melting.

But the man runs off, and then stops, teasing, to turn and call again before disappearing, "Heil Hitler!"

Earringed gypsy men are bent over the bodies of Jews. They are removing shoes and coats, the pockets have already been turned out, papers strewn. They are pulling and rolling off socks and pants. They are stripping the women of what they wear, turning and twisting them this way and that, their hands searching for fastenings. They have found baby carriages to load with their booty, and they are piled high.

He hears a heavy rumbling clattering. It is the sound of the metal rims of the tall heavy-spoked wheels of a heavy loaded cart pulled by a horse slowly across the cobblestones. Shaven-headed convicts are already gathering the dead. It has been done this way at every plague and pogrom a thousand years. The eyes of some of the dead are open, the mouths of some are pursed open like fish that have died in air. Each time the convicts toss a body up into the cart, the bodies already gathered move and jerk, and then, when the cart moves on, the bodies wedge themselves into place, limbs hanging over and through the slatted cart walls.

He enters his cabin, it is lightless, airless. He feels the dog approaching him and he holds out his hand, and he offers his bloody finger to the dog. "Come, Prince, drink! Drink, Prince! Eat!" Why not? And the dog is trembling as dogs tremble avidly before the smell of blood, but the dog will not touch his blood, and in the total darkness he sees the dog's big eyes filled with misery, and now the dog is wailing low like a hurt child.

Three:

I Kill the Beast

1

Malaparte is circling the forest to find his station. He is bullet-headed bald, his sky blue uniform is brushed down, he sits tall and easily in the saddle, but this is a tired old chestnut horse sagging in the middle, its long-necked head hanging. Prince, brown and white mottled, walks along at the horse and rider's side.

He rides in a field between the forest and a castle. It is the moated castle he knows. The countess, he thinks, is in her tower turning over cards still. Prince has stopped behind him in the field, he has raised his head and is looking back uneasily not at the castle but past it.

Malaparte passes station after station and at each a hunter with his attendant, horse and dogs, and now, passing another, he hears from deep inside the forest a bugle call whose piercing notes are muted by distance, and he sees the hunter at his station mount his horse and take his long lance from his attendant and enter the forest. Malaparte has not had to rein his horse, they wait, attentive, near the edge of the forest. He sees in his mind twenty hunters, each with his dogs, entering the forest from their stations. They are armed with lances that arch with their own length and weight. They are advancing slowly into the forest, they hear the shrill trembling cry of the greyhounds on the scent, the fierce yelping of the pack of running dogs; their own dogs racing forward of them, they are drawing the circle tight about the beast.

The bugle sounds twice, the beast has escaped. Somewhere within the forest, Governor-General Frank and his aides, and the captain of the hunt, and the kennel attendants with their fifty running dogs and fifty hounds are galloping in search this way and that, furiously reining here, charging there.

Malaparte takes his station. The attendant waiting for him holds like the staff of a banner the hunter's lance, its steel point longer than a hand. "*Domnule* captain," the attendant says smiling up at Malaparte. Malaparte dismounts. The attendant's hair is short-cropped; he wears a short green peasant's jacket that is too tight for him; Malaparte sees at his waist the bulging form of a pistol.

The horse is grazing, resting; one big eye looks up at Malaparte. Prince is sniffing at the ground. They are standing silent in this field at the edge of the forest; hard blue-violet thorny flowers, and the smaller blue, red, and yellow silken flowers that fade in a day, whose petals, when wet, stick to any passing thing, spot the descending field of high strawlike cereal grass. Jassy and its hills and domes lie veiled in a mist below them. Malaparte turns. The forest overhangs him, tall and dark, the forest dankness chills him. He sees within the forest the sentinel trees, white-barked birch, the bluish spruce that rise tall before branching, he sees the high mass of impenetrable blue growth, the hanging golden veils of autumn leaves, he feels in the stillness that birds are waiting, watching, behind leaves. He thinks that other eyes are watching.

The bugle sounds. Malaparte mounts his sagging-backed chestnut horse. The attendant smiles mockingly handing him the lance. Still, something distant has sounded within the lassitude of Malaparte, the bugle call closer than the last time, louder. He is holding the lance out from his body, he kicks the heels of his boots into the chestnut's belly, and, as the horse jerks forward, he is sighting down the bending lance, the weight of the steel to drop the point into the beast. They have entered the forest and he is conjoint with the horse as with the dog racing at their side, and he is conjoint with the waiting forest, its sentinel trees, and he is the birds waiting, watching, the hundred other eyes. Their pace is a fast trot, the undergrowth whips at the horse's legs. They enter a place of stilled light where tall gray beech rise to vaulted branches far above, and now they enter a low dim forest of black pine, cushions of rotting needles passing beneath the flying hooves of the horse like a thick racing torrent, Prince, at a side, springing, leaping.

Malaparte hears distant hoofbeats. In another part of the forest another hunter is charging his horse forward, his lance ready. They are charging on the spokes of a wheel toward the center. But the wheel itself is turning, the wheel is moving forward. The great hairy beast is at its center, the hundred dogs followed by the captain of the hunt, and the kennel attendants whipping their horses and dogs forward, and Governor-General Frank and all his aides, chasing it. They are tracking their own center and the spokes are turning and the wheel is moving.

He hears hoofbeats from right and left, they are charging in the tunnel spokes of the turning wheel. Now he sees ahead the hunt captain and the attendants waiting, and Governor-General Frank on his tall white stallion, and then sees what he has been hearing all this time, the honey of dogs moiling and yapping about what must be the beast. Malaparte feels the other hunters arriving all about him, each with his lance pointed, the circle forming. And the hunt captain raises his hand like a blessing and command toward Governor-General Frank that he be ready, that he is the King of the Hunt, that he must kill the beast, and the governor-general is staring into the moiling mass with that deepest and even religious concentration of the artist before his moment. So this too has been for a thousand years. And every hunter wanting the kill for himself but observing his place, and every attendant wanting the final nod that he drop to the gored boar's back and slit its throat. And then, when the beast lies bleeding out its black blood, every hunter will come forward to point his lance into the blood and smoking wound of the beast.

There, at the center, is the fiery-eyed enormous black beast. It is backing off on its low legs, inviting the dogs in, and every mounted hunter is tense for his dogs as for himself, the courage of the dog the master's own. But now, as the dogs close in again, the beast, all bunched tight, sprints into a charge, the low legs trampling, and the beast is so low, the long snouted head almost grazing the earth, that dogs leap over his long hairy charging body, and he swings his head up in a sudden arc, his tusks swiping and ripping into a soft belly, and he shifts direction and swipes up again, and all about him dogs are flying and falling, and he swiping up, and hunters are shouting their dogs by their names back at the beast, and the attendants are whipping into the mass of dogs, but the pack force and fury is gone, and even as the hunt captain drops his arm that the sturdy florid-faced governor-general charge the beast now, and the governor-general spurs his horse forward, the beast swings off—horses rearing up, neighing—

and, breaking the circle, is gone into another part of the forest. An attendant shouts curses at the hunters who let the boar through. And again the hunt starts off, the hunt captain leading, Governor-General Frank on his tall white stallion, and his aides, following, and only after a moment, gone from view, does the hunt captain remember to blow his bugle twice again that the hunters return to their stations that the beast not escape the forest.

Malaparte stands in his stirrups peering into the forest where the hunt has disappeared. The high gray striated tree trunks are columns, leafy arches woven above, dust rising in beams across and at an angle to the columns, the light golden, an other worldliness to the filmy insubstantial light. Still, there to a side, the gray trunks of trees are themselves golden, bearing the light. The forest floor billows with great lacy fern, all is slow, cushioned. In the distance, caught for an instant in a beam of dust-rising light, is a gray dog. He moves in a wolflike loping gait, but slow, off, he is hurt. Malaparte is risen on his horse, peering at the wounded wolflike dog, and Prince too is stopped, wide-eyed, watching. The wolflike dog moves this way and that, he has lost direction, he looks up at the leafy arches veiling the sky. Malaparte too looks up. The sunlight glows through a spiderweb of silken filaments, and the light is golden, and he is looking at the delicate crisscrossing filaments, the force of light behind. When Malaparte again looks back down the wolflike dog is sinking into the forest floor.

Again Malaparte is called by the bugle. Again he mounts and takes his lance from the smiling mocking attendant, and again, Prince below, at his side, he rides into the forest. Every almond-shaped leaf is an eye, eyes hang in clusters, and hidden beneath the hanging ferns, as he is shaded by the high leafy arches, are motionless wide-eyed ferrets and wood rats. There is a stillness here so dense it is quivering movement, it rises from the forest floor and is almost visible, the breathing of the forest floor into the caught space beneath the trees; there is a density of stillness here that rises from the thousand-living waiting things, and that hangs far above, crenelate-edged eyes, birds motionless on branches.

Here, trees are silver, and blanketing the forest floor as fern leaves do elsewhere are yellow water lily–like flowers, their petals spread flat as on the surface of water. Malaparte's horse carries him grazingly through the lake of flowers. He thinks of the closing of the flowers, each arching petal drawing the circle closed, slow whirling of circle. He looks up into the forest and the bright flower light is in his eyes yet, and he sees radiant circles, wheels. He hears a whirring movement and then a cawing and sees a giant black bird fly off into the dark distances of the forest. He sees a man standing in the hollow of a tree, a rifle at his chest. A partisan, Malaparte thinks as he rides on as if without taking notice, troubled then by something in the man's appearance.

He enters a place of tall white oak, trees that space themselves large, that, over hundreds of years, construct their grand vaulted arches. All is vast held space here, and the light is dimmed, yesterday's light. He stops, he knows he is followed. He is a big bullet-headed man standing twisted tall in the saddle in this vastly tall forest, his dog too twisted up, searching in the spaces behind. They are differently lit, dimly lit, high rooms, yesterday behind yesterday. Here again is a crater of light, the forest splintered into shards, the trees are hands and fingers sticking up charred black and ash white out of the cinder and ash earth; they are lightning bolt turned back to the sky. The lightning has fallen here, trees glowing incandescent in the rain and wind, falling then into ash. He carries his lance, almost weightless for the balance; his sagging-backed horse advances here slowly on the ash and rotting wood floor of the forest. Elsewhere, other hunters are making their way forward, each on his own trajectory; but the hounds have lost the scent, or they have lost their will, and there is no baying of the beast. He wonders why, if they have lost the beast, the hunt captain's bugle does not call them all back to their stations. He wonders why, if he is followed, Prince does not bark the intruder away. Again he glimpses a partisan, but this time he understands what troubled him before, this partisan's hair, like that of the first, is close-cropped like a convict's or a soldier's.

He thinks that in the forest are circles and circles, he thinks of the widening circles on the surface of still water, of circles interpenetrating circles; he thinks that he understands nothing except that he is here again approaching the center.

He hears shots. He sits in the saddle attentive to the stillness that has fallen everywhere. He hears hoofbeats. A white horse is galloping through the dim forest of vast white oak. Governor-General Frank reins his horse. His big face is pale, his blue-eyed gaze is fixed on Malaparte. Look what they've done to me, his eyes are saying. There is a familiar distance between the two horsemen as if of time. Malaparte sees as in a painting a spreading stain of blood at Frank's shoulder, he sees where the blood has stained red the flank of his pure white stallion.

Now more hoofbeats are approaching. Frank wheels

off. Frank's aides arrive in a flurry; they veer off after Frank. One reins his horse near Malaparte and says, breathless, smiling nastily at him, "It's all right now, the Iron Guard's wiping out the partisans and their accomplices!" Malaparte enters the dark rich green forest of giant live oak. The knotted twisting trees are serpentine-barked, swirling eyes in the dark bark, giant eyes in huge bent elbows. Blood-red roots snake across the surface of the loamy earth, acidlike mossy excrescences foam in rising mist over the space between trees. He sees the dark crenelate-pointed leaves, impenetrable jungle of eyes, black over the penumbra of light. He breathes in the stinking rotting burning breath of the earth that rises from the loam and froth. And the beast is again suddenly there.

Its black coat of spiny hair is slick and filthy with sweat. Its snout is wet and blunt, its short upturned tusks are like dirty overlong teeth, there is a breathless foam at its hanging open mouth. It is looking at Malaparte through blood-veiled eyes. Malaparte is seated tall on the sagging-backed chestnut horse, he must keep a hand tight on the reins, he holds his lance, fine balance, so that its steel tip hangs slightly. He sees the absurd short legs of the beast, the almost tiptoeing pointed cloven hooves. But now the space between him and the beast stretches, breathing, as each contracts for the charge, and, gently urging his horse forward, the heels of his feet whispering to it—the dog, too, valiantly stepping forward—, studying the spot behind the beast's no-neck head forward of its spine that rises then like bristling pointed armor, he remembers the beast's groan that rose up out of the earth.

"No!" It is a shrill command coming from behind.

He turns and sees the acne-faced Iron Guard–uniformed boy shrill as a wing-beating bird running forward in the black-green forest. He has spied on him since he approached the forest, and Prince has been too proud to bark at him. The boy is pointing his short-barreled submachine gun from him to the beast, the high proud cheekboned face of his mother, of Dimitriu himself, and of himself only the idiot way his hair is slicked back across his head.

But now the huge beast, seeing the boy stepping forward of the horse and rider, begins his charge, the cloven-hooved feet trampling, propellering until the cannon itself is hurtling across the steaming loaming open space, the frothing loam and black earth flying in all directions. Malaparte sees the boy's booted foot turning, frail boy and small in black, but the boy's finger is on the trigger and the fear is the shrill cry of hate, staccato screaming of bullets. Malaparte sees the shattering of the black stuff of the beast's snout, and the boy is standing now rooted to the earth, firing into the still but differently hurtling beast, the short legs folded under, braking, the hurtling a braking slide now, the bloody eyes blurring, the mass alone coming, the charge stopping only almost at the boy's knees, the beast's huge and bleeding head rising yet in an infinitely slow hook, the boy changing his charger and again pouring bullets—though now almost straight down—into the dark hairy twitching head of the rising beast, the screaming and thudding sounds caught and echoing in this dark twisted-boughed overhanging place.

I am an old man, prisoner of my son, carrying with Colonel Lupu and six other gentlemen-hunter-dressed men, officers, officials, the hairy bloody beast spread and hung upside down from two lances, blood dripping yet from its torn-open mouth. The limbs of the beast are bound tight to the lances, the head and spiny-haired back almost touch the ground, the tusks tease furrows in the ground. The mass of the black beast fills all the space between me and the other prisoners, and we strain against the weight, the lances digging sharply into our shoulders. Our faces and clothes are bloodied. Flies and wasps cloud about the beast and us, the sagging length of the belly of the beast is mangy black, the pink at its stinking parts crawls with small white worms.

My boy, leading the procession down from the forest, is riding my chestnut horse, carrying my lance. Other mounted Iron Guard officers and soldiers, some SS, are about him and among them, on his tall white stallion, is Governor-General Frank. His shoulder wound has been bandaged, but he is pale and stares wide-eyed ahead. A hand like the hand that closes the eyes of the dead has passed over his face as over Lupu's and their faces are masks. Behind us are more mounted Iron Guard soldiers.

The sky is a rich blue. It is as if a short sudden rain has settled the air and each thing is so much itself in form and color it seems new. Our procession of black-uniformed, belted, Iron Guard soldiers, of SS, the massive rounded haunches of the horses, the long swishing tails, the blood-stained flank of the white horse, we prisoners carrying in a buzzing of flies and wasps the giant stinking black boar, the tired dogs, dappled Prince at my side, passes through un-tended stony fields and orchards, a balding old furrowed field glowing brown—yellow, green, wild blue flowers there that are first like strains but then dazzlingly distinct. I see into the silver gray grooved bark of low orchard trees, shadows and shades of colors, I see so clearly it is like touch.

We are circling Jassy. The procession will enter the

town by the birch tree lined road. Indeed, as we approach the road, Iron Guard motorcyclists join us, flanking us with their powerful big-wheeled machines, revving their motors. Thick-featured men, kerchiefed women, have gathered even here and stand in small groups to watch the triumphant march—the upside-down hairy beast, gentleman-hunter-dressed officers and officials, the sky-blue-uniformed Italian captain portering now, sweating, burdened, some of the Iron Guard soldiers carrying their lances upright like flagstaffs. And, as the procession passes them, the people join it. The birch trees, I see, as we swing to enter their dappled shade, are strangely heavy. We are passing into the dappled shade of the tree-lined road, the points of the lances of some grazing the leaves above, and I see to my right and I see to my left the naked bodies of Jews tied and nailed to these slender trees. I have never seen such pure white. Stains of blood on such white are deep and dazzling like the red of roses.

It is a motorcycle flanked mounted and foot procession that grows as it advances up this dapple-shaded road. The people are waiting here, between slender trees, to join it. Hundreds are waiting ahead. In Jassy, in the square before the Jockey Club, they shall be a thousand, their hands fists.

They have nailed the feet of some of the crucified together and the legs are like closed parentheses, though the hanging bodies' weight and the nail-fixed feet have curved some legs more than others. Here and there, in the white, as if essence of it, discolor is rising in a dark greenish glow. Ahead, my boy, on my sagging-backed chestnut horse, has lowered his lance and bent forward in the saddle to kick off on an angling charge. Other Iron Guard horsemen follow the triumphant boy's lead, lowering their

lances, angling off, and the motorcyclists rev their motors and some allow themselves short energetic spurts, and the horsemen are charging ahead and seem to be grazing the points of their lances against the crucified trees.
I am looking at the crucified boy.
His arms are spread, the wrists of his small fine limp hands tied to limbs of the tree, his weak chest pulls forward, his feet are nailed to the trunk of the tree. His hair is black, his eyebrows. One eye is closed, deep-lidded, and the other is open, but, as I have seen it before, the pupil is, as if even at the moment of his death he was trying to avoid or remember something, swooned up and out.
His white body is woman soft. He has small breasts, his small belly bulges. The wound they have lanced beneath his ribs is a dark mouth.
The feet, awkwardly crossed at the crux of the joining parentheses, are fragile, every toe fine and delicate. The pose of all is outside of touch, the tall bald bullet-headed booted man in his stained sky blue uniform turning from the crucified boy—the open mouth of the wound in the pure white flesh—back to his stinking burden, Prince, at the cross, still looking up, but fixedly below even the nailed feet of the boy.

2

The crescent filament of the wall bulb is like a glowing worm, the light off the concrete walls is harsh. My cell is a cold dank basement room of the Jockey Club.
Distantly, from outside, there is the straggling sound of a salvo of shots. The Iron Guard, with the blessing of

the SS, has taken the power and is executing traitors, purifying Jassy. It is night now, but I know the people are still dragging traitors through the streets to the Jockey Club to try them before the tribunals of insults and fists. In Bucharest, General Antonescu and the army is at the king's right hand, but Horia Sim and the Iron Guard is at his left. And the king is only a boy and Horia Sim has the soft effeminate face even of Himmler. What does it matter that the Iron Guard began to take over Jassy even before the "partisans" fired at Frank? The New Order has taken the power in Jassy and tomorrow everyone will be wearing belted black. And tomorrow the SS will have had their surrogates pay me for my jokes, and after some weeks, the Italian Consul, returned here, will wire to Italy that Curzio Malaparte is reported to have been killed during the recent troubles in Jassy. I have been of the wrong party, I have been, it seems, of the party of Governor-General Frank, and he was too mild, and he loved the Polish people too much, and I have been of the party of Colonel Lupu, and he was not hard or pure enough. And it is true; I feel for them even as for myself.

This room stinks of me. I want pencil and paper. How does it begin, a slow-moving circling ash-painted crouching man, an eye-lidded mask. . . . Does your mother, I shall ask my cross-belted son when he, with his men, comes for me, know what you are doing? My mother, he shall reply, does not care what I do. I shall refuse the blindfold and, standing facing my executioners, I shall cry out, *Vive* Malaparte! I am laughing in my cell, writing a Tartar story.

There is a noise outside my cell. They are coming for me. No, the steps I have heard are not the booted ones of the executioners, and now the door is unlocked and the guard admits to my cell the haloed silver-haired woman, the tall bald servant. I do not believe it is really her, this is only a dream. *Vive* Malaparte, I say to myself to keep my bearings. I too, countess, have a dream. Will you listen to it?

"You must dress in Inre's clothes," she says. "We don't have much time."

"Why?" I ask her, for I merit nothing and this is the holy love I have all my life longed for.

But she will not look at me as if I have long been other than what she thought I was, and I understand then that she has not come to save me but only the boy. "Do you know, countess," I ask, "how the Tartar son kills his father?"

"I don't want to hear."

"When the father is old and weak, the son makes his father into his mother. And so one becomes a man and the other a woman, and they can go on loving each other, all dreams come true."

Still, I am changing clothes with the hairless man and now we call the guard back, and Inre is in my stained sky blue uniform sitting on my cot, and I would, at the entry of the Jockey Club, bid the countess adieu, but she is already gone back into the salons, and the dwarf-small doorman sees me dressed as the emasculate servant and is grinning.

I cross the square before the Jockey Club where fires are smouldering in the night, where the beaten lie groaning next to the unburied dead. I enter my Ford. I turn the key in the ignition, the spark is weak but the motor takes and coughs then like a motorcycle.

The dark cobblestoned streets are barely wide enough for the tall Ford to pass. On such uneven streets, I must negotiate not only the width of the frame of the car, but the swaying sweep of the roof of it. In my dim lights, I glimpse a scurrying of rats across the cobblestones, a reflection of my dim lights in a hundred eyes. The humped cobblestones are moving, swarming; I am driving toward a rising sea of approaching squealing rats. I brake, I shift into reverse, I am twisting to see backward. But there is too little light and the rats are already flooding under the car. I go forward again. They are jumping high as the windows, they twist their furry bodies in air, their long tails slap against the car; they are pressed to the windows and seem to be climbing body on body and when they fall their little clawed hands trail a slime down. They are swarming forward across the curved hood of the motor to the windshield, their small red eyes shining, but hundreds more are coming from behind. They are standing squealing at me, they are making speeches at me. They are squealing and shooting off all about me. I increase the speed, I switch on the bright lights as I enter the broad birch tree lined road. In the white beams of light, against the white of the upright slender striated tree trunks, their bodies greenish and flowering red, the crucified hang in arcs high into the road. The rats in the road here are a wild-moving rabble, but some are poised high on the bare shoulders of the crucified, and where they have plucked out eyes are the small glaring bloody eyes of rats.

I am flying down this alley, my white beams illuminating the far framing trees, the flowering trees shooting off like fireworks into the night as I pass them.

3

Malaparte crosses Europe into Italy in the gypsy caravan of schooner wagons. Long will Malaparte remember the sound of the small bells attached to the heavy plodding gypsy horses, the earringed gypsy men dozing over their reins. All his life, he will honor the Black Madonna, patroness of gypsies. He is in rags and has nothing, and the gypsies take him in and give him clothes and disguise him as one of their own, and every night they make camp outside another town, and every night the officers and top-hatted gentlemen of the town visit the gypsy camp, and there is the hand-clapping foot-stamping dancing, and the gypsy song of pain that rises from the belly and is so exquisite it is almost joy.

In Italy, he tries to contact his protector, Ciano, but Ciano is in disfavor and Malaparte is arrested. This is an old story, a plagiary. One year he languishes in prison, but the Americans have invaded Italy and the king of Italy rallies the Americans and, remembering Malaparte, has him released from prison. The king gives back to Malaparte his rank of captain and makes him his liaison officer to General Smith, Governor-General of Naples.

Malaparte takes visiting American senators to Pompeii, where he shows them the miniature paintings of the indecencies that, he explains smiling, surely brought the catastrophe to Pompeii. He takes them in their straw Panama hats and white summer suits through the labyrinth streets of Naples that stink of open sewers and DDT. Cripples and beggars reach out their filthy hands to the immaculate senators. The senators see American Negro soldiers, their big white-toothed smiles, waiting on lines, shuffling and almost dancing in place, to enter the vast Neapolitan brothels. And one of the senators says to Malaparte, "You Italians have no pride."

Tonight, General Smith is having a dinner party to honor the young hero Audie Murphy. He has invited

French General Juin and his aides; he has invited Colonel Sharp, commandant of the WAC Corps in Naples.

"Fish!" General Smith insists to his aide-de-camp, Colonel Jack Jones. "This Murphy guy is Catholic and today's Friday."

Malaparte says, "There's no fish in all of Naples. In the Bay of Naples, we have floating American, British, and German mines, we have sunken ships, but we have no fish. Your navy has forbidden fishermen to fish that they are Italians and might be spies and bring information to German submarines. Besides, all the Italian fish have been bombed to death. Italian horses, chickens, birds, we can still find some. But fish, that's impossible."

"Impossible, Malaparte, is not an American word," the general says.

"Not even the pope eats fish on Fridays."

"This boy's an American, not an Italian Catholic. And if he wants fish, he'll have fish. Isn't that right, Jack?"

"That's right, sir!" And turning, Jack winks at me that he has something up his sleeve.

General Smith and his twenty guests sit at the long table in the banquet room of the Duke of Orvieto's ancient palace. Above them, above the candle glittering crystal chandeliers is a blue, green, and pink Triumph of Venus painted three hundred years ago by Pietro da Cortona. The waiters are white-gloved, their livery is more elegant than any uniform here; but they have, under this same ceiling, served Spam and corn good only for chickens to their American conquerors. Still, their service is a dance, they move as if on tiptoe.

Colonel Sharp alone is out of uniform. She wears that long evening gown that every American WAC and nurse brings along with her in her duffel bag to Europe. She is no longer a young woman, her face and shoulders are like porcelain. Her eyes are blue, vestal, commanding.

The guest of honor is beautiful. There is no expression on his pure round American-Catholic face that has yet to be marred by a pimple or a hair. He is eighteen years old but is small and fine as a boy. He single-handedly killed one hundred and fifty Germans and took three hundred prisoners.

Audie Murphy is a boy of silence. He will not shine in conversation, or even in modest smiles. His attention is elsewhere. He is a boy listening to his own impossible music a thousand years away. Malaparte wonders if he can even put together a sentence in any language that men speak. He is too pure. What he did on battlefields is, Malaparte knows, a miracle that has nothing to do with the blood and death of real men. It is all a dream only. Malaparte suspects that if the boy ever talks, he will awake and never dream again, that if he discovers what he has really done, he will want to kill ten times as many men. There is distantly, restlessly, about him, as there is haloing every boy, something incomplete.

General Juin is a thick florid-faced man. He was loyal to the German-collaborating Vichy government of Marshal Pétain until a year before when, twenty-four hours after having reluctantly ordered his troops to fire at the Americans landing on the beaches of Algiers, he ordered a cease-fire. Now, though he was a classmate of De Gaulle at St. Cyr, he is backing the Roosevelt-favored candidature of General Giraud for leader of the Free French. His troops are equipped with American arms and are paid with American scrip.

The guests are served on the famous porcelain Monteddio service of the Duke of Orvieto first courses of winged rainbow trout, oysters, a pearl in almost every one. The guests wonder at the magic of this Lenten meal served in candlelight on tiptoe. But Jack, radiant with triumph, replies to every question, "Top secret!"

"Should we eat the pearls?" one American officer asks like asking what fork one should use. The guests look to General Smith, to General Juin, to Jack, to Colonel Sharp. But not even Colonel Sharp dares decide on etiquette.

"In Italy," Malaparte says, "we suck our pearls."

And everyone sucks at his pearl and exclaims at the salty tearlike taste.

When the plates have been removed, General Juin smiles with contentment and, looking from the blank-faced guest of honor to his host, says, "No Frenchman has ever been more heroic than Audie Murphy!" He is, bringing all of French history to bear, honoring the boy, but honoring America too. Indeed the guests feel for an instant the shadowy presence about them of Lafayette and Bonaparte himself. And they raise their glasses of fine Italian white wine and drink to the hero.

"But Audie Murphy," Malaparte then says, "is not a man."

They look at Malaparte with surprise and the beginning of affront. The boy looks inquiringly at Malaparte.

"Audie Murphy's not a man, he's a boy. All heroes are boys and only boys can be heroes."

"If only boys can be heroes," General Smith asks, showing Malaparte off, "what's left a man?"

"A man can always be a general."

Even General Juin, showing his good humor, smiles.

WAC Colonel Sharp says, "Audie Murphy may be a boy, but he's an American boy. Certainly, in this war, there's no Italian hero, man or boy."

Malaparte inclines his bald bullet-shaped head that he

could not agree more. He says, "The bravest Frenchman of all was, *n'est-ce pas, mon général,* Joan of Arc. . . . There are no Italian heroes, men or boys, but with each packet of Lucky Strike a girl brings home, her mother can buy six pounds of bread on the blackmarket. The girls are our heroes."

Colonel Sharp smiles and enunciates slowly as one does for foreigners who are a little absurd in the way they speak or reason, "First you say that only boys are heroes, and then that prostitutes are your heroes."

"America's hero is a boy, and the French hero is a— virgin, and the hero of Italy is the girl with the Lucky Strike. Why shouldn't she be our hero? Do you think Italian girls want to be prostitutes?"

She says placidly, "American women would never do what your women do."

"Then you shall never have an American saint."

She is smiling condescendingly that she is Protestant. She says, "I wouldn't have imagined that you were religious, Captain Malaparte."

"Like Audie Murphy, I eat fish on Friday. But I'm not like the pope who'd have Rome liberated only by Christians. When Mussolini came to power, the pope signed a concordat with him, when the Germans marched into Rome, the pope blessed them, but now, when General Juin's Moroccan troops are waiting outside of Rome for orders to march, the pope sent a company of robed and hooded monks into the French camp to convert them before they enter the Holy City."

General Juin is frowning.

"The general ordered the monks out."

"I hope the pope wasn't offended," General Smith says.

"It was no place for monks," General Juin says briefly. "The general thought the Moroccans might forcibly convert the monks. You needn't have worried, *mon général*, the monks are not twelve- and thirteen-year-old Italian boys."

Everyone is embarrassed at the turn Malaparte has given the conversation except Colonel Sharp who knows all about the immoral traffic of young Italian boys but will resolutely not allow herself to take seriously anything Malaparte says, certainly not when all that is really at issue is Italian morality. She says, "In a moment, you're going to tell us that Italian boys are saints too."

"No, they are angels."

General Smith says, "Malaparte can be a wonderful story teller when he wants. Malaparte, tell Murphy the story of Max Schmeling."

The boy is looking at Malaparte with large troubled eyes.

But now four white-gloved liveried servants enter carrying on their shoulders on a huge silver platter a dark glowing enormous fish. Everyone stretches or rises a little in his chair to see better.

The platter is laid down in front of General Smith.

It is a girl, a child. Her eyes are wide open, her bloated lips seem yet to be breathing. The chefs have circled her with green seaweed. Colonel Sharp has stood in horror, her arms are crossed at her breast, her hands holding on to her porcelain shoulders.

But now the guests see that what might have seemed to be a sequinned dress is even the skin of her body, and that though it gently outlines what might have seemed to be small breasts, a small belly, these are surely fish's breasts, a fish's belly. The fish lies flat, without even a

151

pillow; it is gazing up past the flickering chandelier at the blue sea, the birdlike fish, the peacock-feathered sea-horses of Pietro de Cortona's Triumph of Venus. Malaparte would say, The fish needs only wings to swim home, but even he is speechless.

General Smith demands in a trembling voice of his aide-de-camp, "What in God's name is this?"

"It's a fish," Jack says, smiling apologetically, pale like everyone else. "It's the famous Siren from the Aquarium. It's the rarest and most delicious of all Italian fish."

But Audie Murphy has stood and, his face white as a sheet, is leaning over the siren. He brings his fingertips to the siren's eyelids and closes her eyes. He turns to General Smith and he says, "I think, general, we have to bury her."

"Where are we going to bury a fish?" The general asks because now everyone but the boy has understood that it is a fish, it has short fin-like flat arms, its long flanks end in a fish's tail. "Malaparte," he asks, "where can we bury a fish in Naples?"

"We could bury her in the garden," Malaparte says.

"I think, general, we should bury her in the garden," Audie Murphy says, and there is in his eyes what surely there was when he killed the one hundred and fifty Germans, there is in his eyes that righteous fury of he who has been hurt and betrayed. He is boy-tall facing the general, but there is something blind and all-seeing in him that makes everyone turn again to the siren and give to her the very soul of a child.

They are a strange candlelit dinner party following down the broad entry stairs into the walled rose garden the white-gloved liveried servants carrying on the silver platter on their shoulders the red velvet covered body of the fish with a child's soul. They stand waiting, the candles flickering in the warm wind, as the servants dig a grave in the soft rich earth. The sky is cloudy, still there are long horizontal traces in the sky of the white light of the moon. Outside the garden walls, the hungry dogs of Naples are wailing as if at the deaths of their masters. And here, though no one will pray aloud, General Juin removes his kepi and bows his head. General Smith, ever available to etiquette, does the same, and then so do all the generals' aides. Colonel Sharp wears over her bare shoulders the jacket of an aide, but there is nothing military about her bearing. And in her blue eyes staring past the hero—bent as if he has lost his very sister—at the velvet-wrapped body being lowered into the grave are big round tears. Malaparte begins to laugh. And now everyone turns to Malaparte laughing over the grave of the monster fish who will never again return home to the sea, laughing at the mourning boy and the uncovered generals and the vestal woman. And Malaparte is laughing so hard his knees will not hold him, and he is rocking with laughter kneeling in the rich dark earth that alone can console him.

I return in the night to Capri, and, as I, breathless, slowly climb the mountain path to the ruins of Mon Repos, I see myself standing at my lectern, tall man and big, my bald head bullet-shaped. I am monk-robed, I am writing with a quilled pen, designing in a great book open on the lectern. The pages of my book are illuminated. A man is wrestling with an angel and everywhere about them are flames, birds, beasts.

686666

Samuel Astrachan, a writer and professor of English at Wayne State University, has published four novels: *An End to Dying, The Game of Dostoevsky, Rejoice,* and *Katz-Cohen.* He lives in Gordes, France.

The manuscript was edited by Elizabeth Gratch. The typeface for the display and for the text is Times Roman.

The book is printed on 55-lb Glatfelter text paper and is bound in Holliston Mills' Roxite Vellum. Manufactured in the United States of America.